Dear Journal of an Idiot

—that would be me, Elizabeth Beech, a fifteen-year-old high school student who's done something so stupid she hates to put it down in words (although she seems to really need to. It's why she bought you).

What I need to say right off is that my goal in life is to become a writer. This is not the Idiot part, since I think I do have talent. The Idiot part is that when my teacher, Mrs. Reeves, asked me to submit my writing to an editor—a *real* editor at a *real* publishing house—I went ahead and did it. I sent a sample chapter of a book I'm working on. She wrote me a letter and said she'd like to read more! Good news, right? Wrong. Because I only had the one chapter and I cannot write the rest. Yep, I'd say "Idiot" is the word.

Letters to Julia

BARBARA WARE HOLMES

HarperTrophy®
A Division of HarperCollinsPublishers

Harper Trophy® is a registered trademark of
HarperCollins Publishers Inc.

Letters to Julia
Copyright © 1997 by Barbara Ware Holmes
Printed in the United States of America. For information address
HarperCollins Children's Books, a division of HarperCollins
Publishers, 10 East 53rd Street, New York, NY 10022.

Library of Congress Cataloging-in-Publication Data
Holmes, Barbara Ware.
    Letters to Julia / Barbara Ware Holmes.
        p.   cm.
    Summary: In her journal, chapters of the novel she is writing,
and letters to a New York editor who has befriended her, a fifteen-
year-old budding author reveals her journey of self-discovery in the
midst of a dysfunctional family.
    ISBN 0-06-027341-0. — ISBN 0-06-027342-9 (lib. bdg.)
    ISBN 0-06-447215-9 (pbk.)
    [1. Authorship—Fiction.   2. Family problems—Fiction.
3. Letters—Fiction.   4. Diaries—Fiction.]   I. Title.
PZ7.H7337Le   1997   96-34804
[Fic]—dc20   CIP
                                                                   AC

❖

First Harper Trophy Edition, 1999

Visit us on the World Wide Web!
http://www.harperchildrens.com

For David and Sarah

146 West Cliff Street
Edgewood Heights, NJ 08025
September 30, 1994

Ms. Julia Steward Jones
Editor
Springtime Press
One East 56th Street
New York, NY 10022

Dear Ms. Jones,

My name is Elizabeth Beech, and I am a sophomore at Edgewood Heights High School in Edgewood Heights, New Jersey. Yesterday, my English teacher, Mrs. Reeves, gave me your name. You're the editor of her best friend's sister, a writer named Gillian Watson. Mrs. Watson told my teacher that your press specializes in books for young people and that as an editor you're "generous to beginners." Mrs. Reeves (who was also my teacher last year) immediately made submitting something to you my personal assignment. She thinks I have talent.

I don't know. In my opinion I have a lot

to learn about life and writing. I admire a writer like Henry James. You can tell by his writing that he'd been everywhere and thought about everything and everyone he'd met before he wrote about any of it. I'm only fifteen and I haven't been anywhere. Mrs. Reeves says "leave it to an editor to decide if you have talent" and that "good editors help writers they believe in." That's a nice thought. I agreed to write a query in case she's right. My query is: Would you be willing to read Chapter One of the book I'm working on? I'd appreciate hearing anything you had to say, good or bad. Sometimes it seems to me that my life is filled with two kinds of people—those who only want to say bad and those who only want to say good, no matter what. I could use a true opinion.

Thank you very much for even reading this letter. I'll understand if you answer my query with "no."

Sincerely,
Elizabeth Beech

Springtime Press
One East 56th Street
New York, NY 10022
October 28, 1994

Ms. Elizabeth Beech
146 West Cliff Street
Edgewood Heights, NJ 08025

Dear Ms. Beech:

Certainly you are welcome to send me your chapter. I must warn you, however, that chances are slim it will find a home here. We receive many submissions from young people who have been prompted by well-meaning adults to submit them. Unfortunately, the fact that we specialize in books for children and young adults does not mean that we publish books *by* them. Such books are seldom polished enough to succeed on our list, no matter how great the blossoming talent.

Nevertheless, I shall read your chapter with interest if you choose to send it. And please, extend our regards to Gillian by way

of your teacher. We haven't had anything
new from her in quite a while.

> Sincerely,
> Julia Steward Jones
> Editor

146 West Cliff Street
Edgewood Heights, NJ 08025
November 3, 1994

Ms. Julia Steward Jones
Springtime Press
One East 56th Street
New York, NY 10022

Dear Ms. Jones,

Thank you for answering my letter. I'm embarrassed that I took up your valuable time. I thought Mrs. Reeves (my teacher) would be also, but when she read your letter, she said, "There! Now you have an editor willing to read your writing. Send it!" So here it is, with new apologies.

Very sincerely,
Elizabeth Beech

Chapter One

I WAS TEN YEARS OLD when my family split apart. I don't mean split *up*, I mean split apart. My mother and Eric to the right side of the house, my father and me, Elspeth Nicholson, to the left. As far as I can tell, each of us broke right down the middle when it happened so that we're hollow inside—blank in our centers, like the empty hallway between the halves of the house, or the row of canisters in my mother's kitchen that no one bothers to fill.

I hate being with my father. Only his body is ever here. His mind, if he has one, always lives somewhere else. Once, when I was eleven, I tried to live in the hallway between the halves of the house, but it didn't work out. No bathroom. No food. No privacy, since my mother has to come into the hallway to get to her upstairs. Nothing but muddy boots and old umbrellas and me, tucked into a corner beside the stairs, watching the others come and go. It was almost like being homeless.

So, for six years, minus that short stretch in the hall, I've been with Dad. It's worked out perfectly for my parents—Eric to do the man's work for Mom and me to be the wife. I cook, clean, do laundry. Watch my father sulk.

"Grow up," I tell him (sounding like my mother!), but that only makes him worse. Someday I'll escape for real, to a place with a center that holds more than muddy boots. I know the place too—the *very* place. It's an apartment, occupied at the moment by my friend Angela's sister and her husband. They're saving their money for a house "a year or two down the road." Perfect. When they move out, I move in. That apartment is mine, I know it. I knew it from the very first minute I saw it. Angela's sister, Sammy, was standing in front of one of the huge wonderful windows that run from floor to ceiling, and the sun flashed around her as if she were made of metal. I was dazzled, like a baby when something sparkly and unexpected is dangled in front of its eyes. "Mine!" a voice hollered in my head.

Sammy doesn't have curtains on the

windows and I won't either. "Light is everything," she says, and I mostly agree. Light and air. Space doesn't matter too much. I could live in a one-room apartment and be happy as long as it had a window and nobody else inside it. Funny—I feel suffocated in this whole big house, but I'd feel free in a tiny room.

Not that space isn't also nice—room for pictures and books. Sammy's apartment has a lot of space. It's perfect in every way. Lately, when I have extra money, I buy things for my future apartment. So far, I have a carved candle shaped like a flower to sit on my mantelpiece; blue cloth place mats with matching napkins (for my table that doesn't exist!); and one china teacup. I found the cup in an antique store. The lady who sold it to me said it had lost its value when it lost its matching saucer. Plus it has a chip you can hardly see on its bottom. Doesn't it matter that it also has delicate pink flowers painted on its side and solid gold around its rim? The lady practically gave it away, as if it were nothing.

It's lonely seeing beauty where no one else sees it. Angela doesn't even notice her sister's apartment, and she agrees with my mother that pretty things are just clutter. My mother's philosophy is: if you can't use and abuse it, then throw it away. Or at something. She threw *me* at my father. He isn't fussy.

Twice lately I've visited Sammy when Angela wasn't there. Sammy thinks it's weird, I know, but she lets me in. She looks at me looking. Yesterday she said, "This is a wonderful apartment for someone starting out." Some*one*. If she'd been referring to herself and her husband, she'd have said *people* starting out. I think she knows.

The apartment doesn't come furnished, which is a problem, but I don't care. I'll sleep on the floor if I have to and buy things as I can afford them. So what if I don't have a table? I'll set my teacup on the kitchen window ledge, where it will shine in the morning sunlight.

Someday, when I've made it as a writer, I'll probably want to move—to be in a bigger city where things are more literary. By then I'll have friends all over the world and know where I belong. Until then my apartment will do just fine.

Can my parents come to visit? No, they can't. I'll visit them in their ugly split-down-the-middle house. I'll sit in the center hallway and make them come talk to me together—that dreaded fate worse than death. "My throat's been hurting for weeks," my father will tell my mother. "Try soaking your head," she'll tell him back. I'll simply smile. I'll have a lot to smile about.

Springtime Press
One East 56th Street
New York, NY 10022
December 6, 1994

Ms. Elizabeth Beech
146 West Cliff Street
Edgewood Heights, NJ 08025

Dear Ms. Beech:

Thank you for sending your sample chapter. You shouldn't be embarrassed. Your teacher is right, you do have talent. Even more importantly, you have a poetic sensibility, something rarer than the gift of words. I don't find it in many of the manuscripts that cross my desk, believe me.

I'd be willing to read more—all—of this book, if you wish to send it. While it's unlikely I could actually do something with it, I'd enjoy reading and commenting, in the hopes of being helpful. It would be nice to live up to your teacher's expectations, though I confess I seldom do. In today's fast-paced world of publishing, it's hard to

find time to tend to the new voices. A pity
for all of us.

Sincerely,
Julia Steward Jones
Editor

146 West Cliff Street
Edgewood Heights, NJ 08025
December 10, 1994

Ms. Julia Steward Jones
Springtime Press
One East 56th Street
New York, NY 10022

Dear Ms. Jones,

Your letter has shocked and thrilled and
frightened me. I can't eat or sleep. Luckily it
came only yesterday, so I haven't starved to
death!

Thank you so much for reading and liking my writing. Yours is the first opinion I
can trust. Mrs. Reeves gets so excited by
any sign of life in her students that she
always goes overboard with her praise. I try
to remind myself that what's "exceptional"
at Edgewood Heights High School is not
necessarily "exceptional" out in the world.

Unfortunately, there's a problem. There *is*
no rest of the book. Mrs. Reeves is filled with
disbelief that I sent you the first chapter of a

book I haven't written when I have notebooks full of ones I have, but this is the best writing I've done, I'm sure of it, and now none of my old work seems good enough to send. I thought that by the time an editor asked to see more (should such a miracle ever happen), I'd have new chapters written because I write so quickly. I don't have them written, though.

The problem is, Chapter One is true, as you might have guessed, with only the names of the people changed. And ever since I put it into the mail, whenever I start to write, I think about who I'd be hurting if the book got published. I know this is foolish—no one's book just gets published, the first time they send it out—but now it all seems so *real*. When I start to write, I imagine people reading what I've written and I have to rip things up.

Should I send you my older stories? I don't want to. I want to write and send you this. But I don't want to hurt people either.

I don't know exactly what you mean by "poetic sensibility," or how you can tell I have it from that one chapter, but if it's even rarer than the gift of words, I'm very glad to hear I do! Thank you for saying so.

I'm sorry about the rest of my book. Or my nonbook. Now I've really wasted your time.

Sincerely,
Elizabeth Beech

12/11/94

Dear Journal of an Idiot—

—that would be me, Elizabeth Beech, a fifteen-year-old high school student who's done something so stupid she hates to put it down in words (although she seems to really need to. It's why she bought you).

What I need to say right off is that my goal in life is to become a writer. This is not the Idiot part, since I think I do have talent. The Idiot part is that when my teacher, Mrs. Reeves, asked me to submit my writing to an editor—a *real* editor at a *real* publishing house—I went ahead and did it. I sent a sample chapter of a book I'm working on. Well, dear Journal, the editor liked what she read. She wrote me a letter and said she'd like to read more! Good news, right? Wrong. Because I only had the one chapter and I cannot write the rest. Yep, I'd say "Idiot" is the word.

What I seem to be writing is a book that pretends to be a novel but is really an autobiography. I'd decided to see if I could paint a picture of what life is like with my insane and twisted parents. I thought that if they didn't make sense in real life, they might come clear on paper. But once I put that chapter into the mail, it started to feel like a kind of betrayal. Can you believe it? My parents are acting selfish and being obnoxious and not worrying about me one bit, and *I* feel the guilt. I've had to explain all of this to an editor. How mortifying.

It's also sad because the book is important to me. When I was writing that one chapter, for the very first time I really *felt* like I was a writer. The words just rose up out of me so naturally and amazingly that the world seemed to be snowing words and I had to quick! gather them up with my shovel/pencil before they melted. This has never happened to me before. It was both wonderful and scary and it made my other writing look too lame to even consider submitting it. The editor told me I have a "poetic sensibility, something rarer than the gift of words." (!!!) I'm not really sure what that is, dear Journal, but I think that I believe her. But what good will it do me to have it if I don't feel free to write?

So, dear Journal, that's what I needed to tell you. You'd probably rather be the journal of someone like Kelly, my friend since babyhood, who would write about clothes and boys and record who has been sleeping with whom. Or my mother, who'd have so many interesting neuroses to discuss. She could use you to list all the items she's thrown and broken lately or the things she's accused my father of doing, as if my father could ever stop being totally dull long enough to even imagine what those things are! Well, I'll try to perform a miracle and do at least one interesting thing in the current school year. Maybe hand in a paper late?

12/15/94

Dear Journal of Someone Getting Nowhere Fast,

Well, dear Journal, I decided to give up on the chapters about my family and start a whole other book. But did it work? No, it did not. Because now whenever I try to write, here's what happens: I have a thought that seems like it's worth recording. I turn it over in my mind and admire it from all angles. "Oh," I'll say to myself, "so *that's* my 'poetic sensibility'!" Then I write the thought down, and it seems so perfectly ordinary that I can't stand to read it over. Is it the thought or the words that are trite? I'll ask myself, but I can never answer the question. A real writer could answer that question, I'll think, so I slam my notebook shut.

On the other hand, this weird sort of joy springs up in me now at the oddest moments. Today at school we were reading Shakespeare (*The Merchant of Venice*), and I read these words:

> The man that hath no music in himself,
> Nor is not moved with concord of sweet sounds,
> Is fit for treasons, stratagems, and spoils;
> The motions of his spirit are dull as night,
> And his affections dark as Erebus:
> Let no such man be trusted.

19

And Journal, I knew that I had music in myself. Not music of the literal she-can-keep-a-beat sort, but of a bigger, more important kind. I think what Shakespeare really meant was the ability to be touched by beauty, even though he was talking about music at this point in the play. He meant exactly what I feel when I write something and it's real—that my soul is singing. It is, I can almost hear it. It makes me want to leap out of my chair and run through fields of flowers, just like in those corny scenes in movies, except that in my case there wouldn't be a lover running with me, there would just be me, feeling the music in my soul. And my parents DON'T feel it, that's why they're "fit for treasons, stratagems, and spoils." They are ordinary people, "dull as night." I don't mean this to be braggy, dear Journal, but I'm not ordinary. I have a soul that sings. With work, work, work (and maybe a psychiatrist), I'll be able to write again. Nothing can help my parents.

Dear Journal,

I guess a normal person would be using you to record real things, such as how Christmas is a very depressing and ironic time of year when you have parents who are insane and divorced. And how much it hurts that your best (and only) friend, Kelly, is starting to seem like a stranger.

Not me. All that I care about saying is that I still can't seem to write and right now writing is EVERYTHING—what I'm counting on to get me out of this dump someday. I picture a place where things are beautiful and still and true and the few people you meet when you go outside really listen and say only the things that matter. Writing is a magic carpet that will help me find that place.

Do I sound crazy? I guess I do, but I should confess that to me "crazy" is not a negative word. Unless, of course, it means crazy in the way my mother is crazy, which is truly certifiable! No, "normal" is the nega-tive word if it means being like most of the people I know. This might sound pompous, but it's the way I feel. It's just that no one ever seems to care whether things are interesting or beautiful. Or else their idea of interesting and beautiful is so different from mine that I can't relate. For example: I live in a pretty nice neighborhood, but when I walk to school, I examine the houses and yards and think EVERY ONE OF THEM IS UGLY. I do like one house at the end of McCaw Street where nobody rakes the leaves and the shutters are sunstroke yellow. It's possible a crazy person lives there too.

But I must be a little bit normal because I lied to you before—I do care about those other things. Especially about Kelly, who doesn't walk home with me anymore. I know it's because she's trying out for an opening on the cheerleading squad and has to go home with girls who can help her practice. I shouldn't feel jealous. Still, I can't help noticing how these girls are nothing like me, and that Kelly, walking away with them, looks like a perfect fit.

But you're The Journal of a Literary Person and not a diary, dear Journal, so I'm not going to tell you all that. Or about how my mother stole fifty dollars from my father's wallet and implied that the thief was me. Or how Cathy Petrullo suggested I hurry downtown because they're auditioning Virgin Marys. (Such is what passes for wit at Edgewood Heights High School.) No, dear Journal—to the Journal of a Literary Person that would just be a form of pollution.

12/25/94

Dear Journal of a Scrooge,

If I ever have another Christmas like this one, I will die or kill someone. That's all I have to say.

Or no, it isn't. What I have to say is really a giant question, which I will just go ahead and ask in spite of its being Journal Pollution. The question is this: is there one other family on this entire planet that's even half as bizarre as mine? And now that I've asked it, I may as well answer the question.

The answer is NO, there is not.

My mother and my brother, Roger, came to our side of the house for Christmas. (Yes, our house is divided in half. It's split right down the middle. When my parents got divorced, they hired a carpenter to do it. People seem to find the arrangement a little weird or surprising, but it isn't, really. Not when you see how it works. It allows them to so perfectly torture and spy on each other.)

Anyway, Mom and Roger came over for Christmas, and my brother chose the moment they walked in the door to announce that's he's quitting school and moving to California (in his *senior* year). Merry Christmas. For once I agree with my parents, who've been exploding around the house calling him an idiot and a loser, though I think this may not be the right choice of words for convincing a person to stay in school! "So?" my brother replies. "Then what's the big deal if I quit? I can be an idiot and a loser in California and not have the two of you on my butt besides!" All of which goes to prove he's not such an idiot and a loser and ought to stay in school.

None of us knows my brother. If he's forced to be in the house, he finds a way to hide and never really talks. I can't say I blame him, of course, since he grew up on my mother's side of the house. Nobody living with her would start a conversation on purpose. But still, imagining him moving away is making me feel really lonely. I guess I would *like* to know him before he goes. Part of me thinks I should try to write about Roger—show what his life must be like and why he would want to leave us. The other part thinks that my family's looking more and more pathetic, and writing them down on paper is too sad and dumb for words. Not that I've done any writing.

12/31/94
New Year's Eve

Dear Journal,

My New Year's resolution is to pretend I don't know this family. To use my imagination to cook me up a new one that lives in a totally different house in another part of the world and then to manage to GO there. I see us already: my mother the brilliant writer, who tends to get absentminded and forget about things like laundry but whom we all love because she's lively and loving and such an important thinker. And my father, a gentle doctor, who doesn't the least bit care if my mother's a little flaky. "Follow your star, honey" is all he tells her. "*We'll* do the laundry." (The "we" is me and my younger brothers and sisters.) So we all do the laundry together and make it fun, and since we're rich, we don't even care if things shrink. In fact, sometimes we *try* to shrink things or to make the colors run, just for the sake of experimentation. "Hmm," my father will say. "Interesting permutation."

Or maybe I'll live alone in a cozy room in New York City and hang out with artists and writers. They'll want me to go to foreign movies and visit art museums and discuss what I've been reading. "So what's it like being an orphan?" they'll sometimes ask, and I'll have to tell them the truth: "It's just heaven."

The news from the real world (Pollution Alert) is that my brother's decided to stay in school. He says the minute he graduates, he's leaving for California. I can't say how I feel about this (his staying or his going) because I guess I don't really know. Yesterday I tried talking to him when I was at my mother's, and he looked at me like I was speaking some foreign language. Maybe I was. Maybe I always am, at least when it comes to Roger.

Oh well. Happy New Year, dear Journal, but don't really expect one. Your year can't be any better than mine is, and the truth, when I'm not imagining, is that things don't look so good.

Springtime Press
One East 56th Street
New York, NY 10022
January 3, 1995

Ms. Elizabeth Beech
146 West Cliff Street
Edgewood Heights, NJ 08025

Dear Ms. Beech:

You haven't wasted my time. I understand and find it unusually kind of you to care so much about the feelings of people who have obviously hurt you.

Have you considered turning your autobiography into fiction? Try putting your book into the third person and inventing characters to stand in for the real ones. You might feel freed from the constraints both of worry that you will hurt feelings and of the limiting nature of fact. If you're clever about it, people might guess, but they won't know, will they? Have you written any fiction?

I guess it was your depiction of a character who sees and appreciates beauty where no one else sees it that made me say you had a poetic sensibility. The need to capture and express what the rest of the world can't or won't see is a major driving force of an artist. To have discovered and expressed this need by age fifteen is a promising sign. Now that I know the main character is you, I'm even more convinced.

I'll be happy to read anything at any stage of the writing.

Sincerely,
Julia Steward Jones
Editor

Oh My God, Dear Journal,

I've had a letter from the editor who says
I haven't wasted her time. Who says it's
unusually kind (as opposed to stupid) to
care about the feelings of people who've
obviously hurt me. Who says that the need
to capture and express what the rest of the
world can't see is THE MAJOR DRIVING
FORCE OF AN ARTIST. Dear Journal, by
"artist" she meant *ME*. She thinks all I have
to do is try turning my autobiography into
fiction and I'll be able to write the book.
Maybe she's right, too, because while I was
reading her letter, my soul started singing
again and a million ideas rolled into my
head.

So Happy New Year again, dear
Journal!! This time I really mean it.

146 West Cliff Street
Edgewood Heights, NJ 08025
January 8, 1995

Ms. Julia Steward Jones
Springtime Press
One East 56th Street
New York, NY 10022

Dear Ms. Jones,

I think your advice is perfect. I have written fiction, but only *real* fiction, that didn't have anything to do with what was going on with me at the time. It was either Fiction or it was Truth. This will be like combining the two, I guess—expressing how I feel about things that have actually happened, but without describing the true events or the people involved. I'll have to create new people and new events that are both different from and like the real ones. Right?

I feel so honored by your interest in me when you must get hundreds of letters every day from much better writers. If it's true that I have the driving force of an artist, I hope it drives me in the right direction. It's scary, as if whatever it is that's special or different inside of me has to be pulled up very very carefully or it will get hopelessly tangled and not ever appear. Does that make sense?

Thank you so much for writing to me again. I hope I'll have something to send you soon.

Very, very sincerely,
Elizabeth Beech

Dear Journal,

Oh, my poor wrists and fingers! I've been typing, typing, typing, trying to write a new chapter that's fiction but also not-fiction. I can't really judge if it's any good, but it seems to feel right, as if I'm at least headed in the right direction. I've created a mother who is exactly like my mother, who's doing things my mother has never done but would do in a minute if she happened to think of them. And my character Elspeth is me but also not me. It's as if I can let her think any old thing she pleases, and she just happens to choose to think like me. It's very strange and I'm not doing well at explaining, but believe me IT IS EXCITING. That's all you have to know. Dear Journal, I'm finally writing.

Dear Journal,

Life will never be perfect (as if you didn't know). Kelly came over after school, which made me happy, but then, while I was out of the room, she read my newest chapter without even asking, which of course made me mad. Luckily you were in a drawer, or she'd probably have read you too. Honestly, sometimes Kelly is like an elephant. She says whatever comes into her head and looks at whatever is there in front of her without really thinking about what she's doing. If the world gets flattened while she's barging through it, well, hey, that's fine with her.

"Wow!" she said when I came back to the room. "This is great! Are you going to have the father really cheat on the mother with her best friend?"

I grabbed the pages out of her hand and said, "None of your business!" She looked hurt, but I don't care.

"Jeez," she said. "I was only paying you a compliment. Sorry if you find that offensive."

Yes, dear Journal, offensive is what I found it. I have a new favorite word: tedious. Life—and people—can be so tedious. Certainly Kelly can.

Springtime Press
One East 56th Street
New York, NY 10022
January 17, 1995

Ms. Elizabeth Beech
146 West Cliff Street
Edgewood Heights, NJ 08025

Dear Elizabeth:

I'm glad you're excited about your writing. You've understood my suggestion exactly. The best writers do just as you describe: they create fictional characters and situations to stand in for and express emotions and insights they've gained in real ones. The new version may be so removed from the first that even the artist can't track it back to its source, but it *does* have a source or else it isn't honest. It's honesty you're speaking of when you worry about the artist inside of you coming up untangled. Believe me, you needn't worry, she's so close to the surface already and you're nothing if not honest.

No, I don't get hundreds of letters from

writers better than you. I get hundreds of
letters from mediocre talents with superior
egos, and I have to answer every one.
Writing to you is becoming a distinct and
unique pleasure.

I wanted to let you know that I have to
be out of the office for a while attending to
personal business. Needless to say, things
will be backed up when I return. Should you
send a chapter, I'll do my best to give it
prompt attention. Silence means only that
I'm not yet back.

Good luck.

Sincerely,
Julia Steward Jones
Editor

Dear Journal,

You probably didn't know it, but writing to me "is a distinct and unique pleasure," especially for someone who has to put up with so many "mediocre talents." Oh, my God, dear Journal, I actually got a letter from an editor saying those words. When I read them, I thought I would have to lie down on the floor and just die from being so happy.

But now an hour has passed and I want to lie down on the floor and just die period. This person, a professional who is sick of mediocre talents, is expecting a chapter from *me*. I have one, too—one I've worked on over and over until I thought it was pretty good, but now that I have to actually put it into the mail, I think I hate it. I considered showing it to Mrs. Reeves, but that makes me nervous also. It's like I've bled all over the pages, and now whoever gets to read them is going to see some wounded but very real part of me. I guess that's why I overreacted with Kelly, if I did overreact. I guess I probably did since in the past she always read the things I wrote. I tried to think if it meant anything to me that Kelly had liked the chapter, and I discovered that it did, quite a lot. But I don't think I can trust her opinion in the literary sense. I can't even trust my own. Who am I to know what's good enough for an editor?

Okay, dear Journal, I know what you're thinking: editors don't expect perfection because that's what they exist for—to help you with your writing. Right? Right. So what I should do is just give myself one more week to polish up the chapter and then put it into the mailbox, no matter what. And once I've mailed it, I should forget all about it and start working on a new one, because that's what any real artist would do. Right again, right? You're very wise, dear Journal. Thanks for the advice.

146 West Cliff Street
Edgewood Heights, NJ 08025
January 28, 1995

Ms. Julia Steward Jones
Springtime Press
One East 56th Street
New York, NY 10022

Dear Ms. Jones,

Well. I wonder if you're back and if your
personal business is taken care of and if
you're buried under all those letters you hate
to read. Believe me, I'll understand if you
take a long time to reply.

Here's the new chapter. I've been working on it over and over, trying to make it
perfect. It isn't, but for now it's as good as I
can get it. Writing it this way was much
harder and slower, but also more interesting.
I showed it to Mrs. Reeves, who nominated
me for the Pulitzer Prize on the spot. The
woman may be a wonderful person and
teacher, but she just isn't useful as a critic.
(It's only her second year of teaching, which

probably explains things.) I hope you will be a critic. I want to learn and get better and better.

Sincerely,
Elizabeth Beech

Chapter One

ELSPETH'S MOTHER STUCK OUT her ankle and stared down at it, meaning for Elspeth to do the same. Bulletin from the injuries front, Elspeth knew. Her mother had injuries the way other people had breakfast—regularly, but with more enthusiasm on the weekends, when there was time to really enjoy it.

"What's wrong with it?" Elspeth dutifully asked.

Her mother looked up, amazed. "It's swollen! You can't see it?"

Elspeth sighed and bent a little closer. The usual tug-of-war set to work inside her: her mother was a child, deserving scorn—her mother was a victim, deserving pity.

As usual, pity won the war. "I guess I can," she said.

Her mother pulled the ankle away. The leg of her jeans dropped over it. "It's all your father's fault."

Elspeth stared. How could it be her father's fault? Elspeth and her father lived next door, but her parents never saw each other. They hadn't spoken in years, except through Elspeth.

"It's true! I fell on your father's steps."

"You were over at Dad's?" Elspeth couldn't believe it, couldn't begin to guess what it might mean.

Her mother stomped into the kitchen, her swollen ankle forgotten.

"Mom?" Elspeth followed. "What were you doing at Dad's?"

Her mother's chin trembled and then shot up. "Spying, if you must know. Your father had a date."

Elspeth blinked. So? Her father often had dates. "Who's he boring this time?" was all her mother ever said.

"When do you mean? Last night?" She'd slept at Angela's house. She tried to remember what her father had planned to do.

Her mother nodded. Her mouth twisted into a funny shape. "It was Patsy," she managed to say. The words sounded sort of strangled.

"Patsy?" Elspeth was speechless. Patsy was her mother's best friend. "Are you sure?" It couldn't be. Patsy would never do that. Would she? "What were you doing? Looking in the windows?" Had she caught them—at something?

"No." Her mother looked defiant. "But only because I couldn't. I twisted my ankle and had to come home." She stuck out the ankle again.

This time Elspeth studied it with more sympathy. It did look a little swollen. There was a black bruise, right by the anklebone.

"Why don't you soak it?" she suggested.

Her mother nodded and hobbled off towards the bathroom, as if the very ankle that had supported her only seconds ago would break if her foot touched ground.

"How do you know they were dating?" Elspeth asked from the bathroom doorway while the ankle soaked. "Maybe Patsy—had some sort of business." Not likely, she knew. But her mother brightened at once.

"Maybe! I mean, they weren't holding hands, you know?"

Elspeth nodded.

Her mother pulled her ankle from the water and dried it off. She stood up firmly, as if the ankle were good as new.

"Find out for me, Elspeth," she said, sounding almost cheerful. "Go over there right this minute."

"You want me to spy for you," Elspeth said flatly. It wasn't even a question.

Her mother smiled and passed by. "Of course," she called as she disappeared into her bedroom. "You always do."

Her father wasn't home. Elspeth looked around his bedroom for signs of Patsy. There were none. She sighed, hating herself and hating her mother and father.

She didn't hate them, of course, but she hated how they lived, so wrapped up in anger and petty meanness all of the time. In her own bedroom she opened her dresser drawer and pulled out the notebook where she copied poems and sayings she liked, to remind her that somewhere the world was different. Somewhere people thought about things that mattered and tried to put good into the world. Yesterday she'd copied this:

To make us feel small in the right way
is a function of art. Men can only
make us feel small in the wrong way.
                              —E. M. FORSTER

Elspeth closed the book. Suddenly she was
too tired to read one more word. If she read
for hours, she'd still only feel small in the wrong
way. Thanks to two you-know-whos.

Dear Journal,

It's me, Crazy Person, again. Just when
you thought we were headed for rich and
famous—or at least poetic—back comes
crazy. Believe me, I'm more disappointed
than you.

I promised myself I wouldn't think about
my new chapter once I sent it off, but I
can't think of anything else. Or I do think of
everything else, and since I can't stand my
life, I go back to thinking of writing. But I
can't write until I know what Julia Steward
Jones is thinking. Why? If there really is an
artist inside me, why isn't she pounding her
way out without caring what anyone thinks?
It's like she's embarrassed to show her face
unless she's sure someone is going to pat her
on the head and love her.

But I know why, of course. Because no
one around here would understand who she
was. Dad, the corporate accountant? Ha!
He'd stomp on her like a bug. Mom would
laugh. Kelly would roll her eyes. She might
like my stories, sure, but she wouldn't

understand a word I was saying if I talked about anything but their plot lines. She's never thinking of what things mean, in their essence.

Sometimes I think Kelly's sister, Shana, might understand. When we go over there, she gives me these funny looks, as if she'd like to tell me something, and she seems kind of sad in a way I recognize. I think I'd never be sad if I had an apartment like hers, but of course she has a husband who lives there with her, so how can I say what she feels? I do know she knows about beauty— look how she's fixed her apartment.

What I need to do is write something so perfect that other writers will read it and want to share their ideas with me. They'll want to come visit my apartment and talk about books and have coffee. But how can I write something perfect while I'm living in this place? I can't, at least not without help from outside it.

In my last letter I told Ms. Jones to be critical and honest. I meant it, too. But underneath the criticism I need her to love my writing even more than Mrs. Reeves does. If she doesn't, I don't know what I'll do. Being crazy will not be enough.

2/15/95

Dear Journal,

Well, at least I'm writing again. When my mother opened the upstairs window and actually threw a shoe out of it (one of my brother's—she said his ability to wear the same old moldy sneakers a hundred days in a row had driven her to it), I decided that I'd better get to work. Not having an outlet for craziness can be very dangerous (not that I'm ANYTHING like my mother). My brother left the sneaker in the front yard and went to school in one sneaker and one work boot. I think he had the other work boot in his backpack, but my mother didn't know it. She followed him down the driveway in her housecoat yelling at him to get back in the house and put on matching shoes and to stop acting like an idiot. Well gee, yeah, he might embarrass the family.

Dear Journal,

So where IS this editor? And why does reading one little chapter have to take her almost a month? And why does Roger seem to be suddenly working so hard at making Mom insane when he'll be escaping in just a few months? And why do Kelly and I have to keep having fights? It is absolutely not true that I was happy she didn't make cheerleading back in—whenever it was she tried out! It might be true that I didn't think enough about it, or that I secretly thought it was stupid to *want* to be picked, but I would never be happy about something that made her sad, and I told her that. But this is all petty stuff, not worth recording. I'm sorry I just recorded it.

One good thing—I've written a whole Chapter Two and now I'm working on revising it. I think it's better than the first one. Being tense and worried and mad at everybody I know has given me some sort of weird new energy. But what good will it do to have a chapter written if nobody wants to read it? WHERE IS THIS EDITOR??

146 West Cliff Street
Edgewood Heights, NJ 08025
March 9, 1995

Ms. Julia Steward Jones
Springtime Press
One East 56th Street
New York, NY 10022

Dear Ms. Jones,

I promised myself I'd be patient and do
what you asked—just believe silence means
you're not back. But yesterday I looked at
the date of your last letter and saw that it
was January and knew you must be back. I
couldn't sleep all night, thinking how you
had to have read my chapter by now. I'm
afraid you didn't like it and don't know how
to tell me.

I've been working on Chapter Two. It's
hard, not knowing how you like the first one,
but I decided a real writer wouldn't just sit
around worrying and wait to be told what to
do. I won't send it, though, until I hear from
you and am sure you want to see it.

Please don't worry about telling me the truth, even if it's bad. I can take it. I'll only be sorry if I've disappointed you and wasted more of your time.

Sincerely,
Elizabeth Beech

Dear Journal of a Liar,

I *can't* take the truth if it's bad. In fact, I can't take anything bad at all. Not if it comes from a real editor.

Dear Journal,

Math test tomorrow (Happy Birthday to me), so there's really no time to write. I just wanted to say that there's nothing to say in case you were wondering.

Dear Journal,

Today was my sixteenth birthday (yes, as in The Big One—perhaps "Sweet Sixteen" party?). Well, here's what happened to me: Kelly gave me a sweater, which you might think sounds nice but was borderline insulting since she knows how I hate to get clothing; Dad gave me a watch, when I already have a good one; Mom gave me a gift certificate to the Gap (this *was* insulting); and Roger gave me nothing. Mom and Roger came over for supper and brought lasagna and one of those lame frozen cakes. I suppose mine *was* special since it was still semifrozen.

After dinner we all proceeded to have a huge fight based on the fact that Dad will not let me or Roger get our driver's licenses until after we're out of high school. He says there's plenty of time for driving later in life and that teenagers are high-risk drivers and that since we don't have an extra car in the family there's really no point. Roger told Dad he'd already gotten his license without any help from a useless father and stormed out of the house. So then of course Mom and Dad had to have one of their loudest fights ever, since Dad assumed Mom knew all about Roger's deception and supported it and she said how typically insulting of him and he said well she deserved to be insulted

because if she didn't know then she should
have and doesn't she fulfill any role as a parent? Etc. etc. etc.

So. Happy Birthday to me.

146 West Cliff Street
Edgewood Heights, NJ 08025
April 12, 1995

Ms. Julia Steward Jones
Springtime Press
One East 56th Street
New York, NY 10022

Dear Ms. Jones,

I hope it won't seem rude, but I'm sending Chapter Two after all. Believe me, I'm
not trying to rush you. I decided if you
haven't read Chapter One, you might as well
read them together. Also, in one of your letters you did say you'd be happy to read anything at any stage of the writing.

I'm making myself not worry anymore. I
know you're just really busy. I only hope
you like my chapters when you finally have
time to read them.

Sincerely,
Elizabeth Beech

Chapter Two

HER FATHER CAME IN AFTER TEN. Late for him on a Sunday. He stuck his head through her doorway and waved. He looked unusually happy, too.

"How's tricks?" he asked, as he always did.

"Fine." Elspeth fought her usual impulse to bury her head in her book and will him away. "How are you?"

"Great!" Her father came into the room. He fingered one of her old stuffed dolls, then arranged it carefully on top of an opened book on her desk, as if it were reading. Elspeth hated when her father invaded her space, but she couldn't complain. Only minutes ago she'd torn his room apart, looking for Patsy clues.

"So what's new?" he asked.

Elspeth closed her book. "Not much. What's new with you?"

An indescribable look flitted across his

face. A closed yet ebullient look. Was it the look of someone with something to say, or someone with something to hide? He didn't reply.

"Well?" Elspeth prodded. "How was your date last night?"

Her father's mouth fell open. "Date?" His eyes darted around the room.

"Didn't you have a date?" Elspeth loathed herself for the innocent lilt to her voice. When had she gotten so good at this?

Her father cleared his throat.

"Actually—" He cleared his throat again. "Well, truth is—"

Elspeth waited. She couldn't believe it. He was really going to tell her. And it was really true.

He cleared his throat again. "I've been seeing Patsy," he blurted out. His face turned red, then pale, then red again.

Elspeth's ears began to burn. She'd known it, of course. In her heart she'd been sure. But hearing it said was something else.

"Patsy?" At least she looked properly shocked.

"I know, I know," her father said. He looked miserable, and she felt a fleeting burst of pity. "Your mother will hate it. Patsy's concerned about that."

"Well, gee whiz, Dad, no kidding!" How could Patsy be so stupid? How could Patsy listen to years of her mother's complaining and still want this man?

"We didn't plan for it to happen." Okay. Give her father credit. He looked truly concerned. "It's hard for Patsy too, you know."

Hard for *Patsy*? Is that what he'd said? "Yes." Elspeth nodded. "I can see that it might be a little stressful to dump on your lifelong friend. Yes, I do. It could make you very nervous, in fact."

Her father suddenly scowled. "I hate it when you're sarcastic," he said. "I try to tell you things and you get sarcastic. Then you wonder why we can't talk."

"Maybe we can't talk because what you say disgusts me!"

Her father glared at her for a minute, then he turned and walked out of the room.

Elspeth flung her book at the door. She

hadn't handled it right. She'd blown her chance to hear any further news—to *really* know about Dad and Patsy. But she didn't want to know. Not even for her mother's sake.

God, her mother. How would she tell her mother? Elspeth buried her head in her hands. Patsy had been her mother's best friend since childhood. It was Patsy who'd stuck by her mother through the divorce, advising her to stay in the house so her father wouldn't get it. Patsy who'd helped defend her mother's turf when Dad had wanted the table and chairs and couch when he'd bought the house next door.

Her mother had no one else. Only her children and Patsy and the endless men who flitted in and out of her life. The men never stuck, and the children didn't count. Elspeth lived with her father, and Eric was never home now that he had a job.

It was clear. Elspeth would have to move in with her mother. How could she live with her father if Patsy was here? She moaned out loud. It meant the end, of course. The end of all the plans she'd made for her escape after graduation. Her mother was a giant sucking vacuum and Elspeth was only a little dust ball, swirling in the corner. In a short matter of time, *whoosh!*, she'd be gone.

Dear Journal,

Ms. Jones hasn't returned Chapter One (hasn't *written* to me in months!), so what do I do? I send her a Chapter Two, as if MORE might doubly impress her! Fool. I told her I wasn't trying to rush her, but I was, of course, and she'll know it, too. Sending her a new chapter was supposed to make her think about me again. And I guess it will, but don't I care what it *is* she thinks? The really dumb thing is that now she'll take even longer because she has more to read.

That's not the only dumb thing I've done either. Yesterday was Good Friday so we had the day off from school. I was home alone and feeling kind of lonely. Kelly had gone off to be with her father and *my* father had gone to work because that's all he ever does, even on holidays, and Mom was off cleaning some doctor's office, which she has to do when it's closed. Suddenly I got this urge to go and see Shana, Kelly's sister. I felt so stupid when I got there, because of course her husband was home from work.

I'd completely forgotten he'd be there. They invited me in, then looked at me like "Well? So what did you come here for?" I told some lie about just being in the neighborhood and wondering if I'd left my raincoat the last time I'd been there with Kelly. They said no and I hurried back to the door. It was weird—Shana looked at me strangely when I was leaving, as if maybe she'd like me to stay, but she didn't say anything, so how could I be sure? And I didn't ask her.

Why can't you just say what you want to say in life? You never can, really, can you? Except to your journal. So, dear Journal, I'm glad I have you, even if I've polluted your pages by telling you all of this everyday stuff. There'll be more for me to tell you, too, because I'm going to keep marching forward in the dumbness department, I can just tell. One of these days my fingers are going to start typing a begging letter to Ms. Jones and I won't be able to stop them.

146 West Cliff Street
Edgewood Heights, NJ 08025
April 17, 1995

Ms. Julia Steward Jones
Springtime Press
One East 56th Street
New York, NY 10022

Dear Ms. Jones,

I'm sorry to keep on writing, but now I just can't help it. Where are you? Maybe you're still away, the way you said you'd be. But are you coming back? I wonder if you ever got my chapters or will ever see this letter. Well then, will whoever *does* see it please just check one of the boxes on the enclosed postcard and send it back to me?

Thanks! And I'm sorry I sent Chapter Two before you asked me to. It was a childish thing to do. (Like writing this letter!)

Sincerely,

Elizabeth Beech

Ms. Jones is here and swamped with work. ❏

Ms. Jones is not back but is returning soon. ❏

Other (please explain!) ❏

_____

_____

_____

_____

Springtime Press
One East 56th Street
New York, NY 10022
May 1, 1995

Ms. Elizabeth Beech
146 West Cliff Street
Edgewood Heights, NJ 08025

Dear Ms. Beech:

I'm taking the liberty of writing to you in
Julia Steward Jones's absence. Ms. Jones has
been unexpectedly sidetracked by her personal problems and will not be returning to
the office for a while.

I do find your two submissions—one
dated January 28 and the other April 12—in
the pile building up on her desk. Wherever
possible we've assigned manuscripts to other
readers; however, we haven't done so in
your case as there was clearly prior communication between the two of you.

We've now forwarded your recent
inquiry on to her, and she'll no doubt
respond to it directly. If not, please feel free

to contact us again and we'll assign you
another reader.

Sincerely,
Lorraine Bridgeman
Editorial Assistant

449 Ramblewood Road
Roanoke, VA 24015
May 8, 1995

Dear Elizabeth:

I've just gotten your letter of panic with its clever postcard enclosed. I'm sorry to have disappeared on you. Life has gotten very complicated for me, I'm afraid, as I have elderly parents in Virginia and have had to spend most of this year flying back and forth tending to their problems. Your first chapter arrived at the height of my commuting, and I confess to dropping it onto the pile of things that could wait, no offense intended.

Unfortunately, things here have recently gotten worse. In April I came home to be with my mother while she underwent minor surgery, and minor surgery became major surgery and my mother didn't survive. Now my father's ill also. I've been back to New York a couple of times, but only to attend to the most pressing matters. I'm afraid I avoided the mountain I saw on my desk.

Anyway, I'm sorry. I've asked Lorraine to send your chapters. Good news that there's more than one. I'll do my best to read them promptly. By now you've probably written many more. If so, feel free to send them to me in Virginia. And you never need my permission to submit new chapters. I'm happy that things are going so well.

With apologies and
best wishes,
Julia Jones

May 11, 1995

Ms. Julia Jones
449 Ramblewood Rd.
Roanoke, VA 24015

Dear Ms. Jones,

I'm so sorry to hear about the awful
things that have been happening to you. I
never would have bothered you if I had
known. Please, please, don't rush to read my
chapters. I was just writing to make sure you
were out there. I can wait. Don't even worry
about writing to me. Just take care of yourself and your father. You can let me know
when you're back in your office, and I'll
write to you then.

In sympathy,
Liz Beech

P.S. Do you prefer to be called Julia Steward
Jones or Julia Jones? Sometimes you sign
your name one way and sometimes the
other.

Dear Journal,

I bothered Ms. Jones when she was taking care of her dying parents. The whole office at Springtime knows that I bothered her, too. Why did I have to be so impatient? I feel like a child, and a fool.

But even worse than that, now I've written and told her not to worry or even think about me. Journal, WHAT IF SHE DOESN'T? How long can I wait? Not long, because I *am* impatient. I *am* a child and a fool. I want her to read my writing, and I want her to read it SOON because who else is there to care? Not Mrs. Reeves, who is just too weird lately. She's gone from asking me ten times a week whether I've heard from my "editor friend" to looking blank when I mention Ms. Jones. And she frowns a lot and says things like "*if* I come back next year." Well, why wouldn't she come back when she claims to adore teaching and has only been doing it for two years? I asked her if she was moving, but she just looked startled and said, "Oh good grief, no!" and didn't volunteer anything more. It's as if we're strangers all of a sudden.

I've been trying to get inspired by doing a lot of reading—what Mrs. Reeves calls "the Greats." I've read one book by Thomas Hardy, two by Charles Dickens, and more Henry James. It isn't working, though. I keep thinking: what if *they'd* read my chapters? Of course, they wouldn't have bothered. A sentence would have been enough to bore them silly. It makes me feel stupid to know that even if I work for years, I won't ever be as good as they were a century ago.

Where do I fit in? Not here in New Jersey with my own family or even with Kelly, my "best friend." But also not out there, wherever that is, because I don't know enough and maybe I never will.

If only Ms. Jones would keep on liking my writing and encouraging me so that I could learn what I need to know. I'm not a religious person, but I keep thinking, Please, God! Oh please.

Dear Journal,

I'm sorry I haven't written. My father is making me look for a summer job, which is taking all of my time and attention since of course we're doing it his way. HE reads the newspaper want ads and talks to people at work, then makes me go to the weirdest places. I've been to one insurance company (believe me, one is enough), a Burger King (no comment needed), a factory where they make some metal part I don't even know the name of and can't explain its purpose, and a moldy old grocery store where nobody ever shops. I told my father I'd like to work in either a bookstore, a library, a pet shop, or a garden center, and he said, "You and the rest of the world. You'll work where you find a job." Isn't he just the best? He won't even let me commute to Philly, where I might meet someone exciting, heaven forbid.

At least if I'm working, I won't have so much time to think about waiting to hear from the editor. Not that I have time now between school and applying for jobs and cleaning my father's house. I suppose when Roger moves to California, I'll become our yard person too. Oh well. Who needs to hear from an editor when you don't have time to do any writing?

> Yours
> (and everyone else's),
> Liz

Dear Liz,

Thank you for your letter and your sympathy. Please don't feel you're bothering me by writing to me here. I could use diversion.

I've read your two chapters. Congratulations—they're a very good beginning. I'm impressed at how well you've reimagined your characters and turned a first-person narrative into a third-person novel that is a showing and not a telling. You're adept at dialogue and pacing. Your characters come through loud and clear, and Elspeth's sad position between them is very well drawn. Wonderful, that image of the giant sucking vacuum!

It's interesting that you find this kind of writing more challenging. I think it is. To me fiction is a higher art form than pure autobiography, just as, in my opinion (and this has been widely debated), a painting by Matisse is a higher art form than the finest of photographs. Imagination widens our scope and touches at higher truths.

Keep the chapters coming and send

them here. My father needs to be placed in a nursing home and I'm in pursuit of one. It's been harder than I could ever have imagined, watching my parents grow old and ill and knowing no amount of effort can keep them from finally going. There are things in life we can't control—why has this simple truth caught me so by surprise?

Sincerely,
Julia

P.S. I'm either—Julia Jones or Julia Steward Jones. Steward was my mother's maiden name, and I have a sentimental attachment to it. I generally use it in business. But please, just call me Julia. I feel we're becoming friends. And I gather you prefer Liz to Elizabeth?

Dear Journal,

You are now the Journal of a Friend of an Editor! The Journal of a Person Who's Adept at Dialogue and Pacing! I keep thinking, Thank you, God. Thank you forever and ever. But then I go from excitement to shock and fear that this all must be a kind of mistake. What if Julia sees more in my writing than is really there and one day she'll suddenly know it? I'm only a teenager and she's a professional editor who knows about "higher truths."

Julia's right about one thing—I am adept at pacing. I've been pacing my room all night! And what exactly *is* pacing anyway?—of the Julia kind, I mean. And what wild miracle or accident of fate allowed ME to have it?? And please God (or Master of My Fate or King of All Accidents), since you chose to give it to me, will you now let me keep it? I'll work anywhere this summer, even in Burger King, if I know one day I'll be a writer.

Dear Julia (thank you!),

I love that you think we're becoming
friends. I love everything about your letter,
especially what you said about fiction and
painting being higher art forms. I had to
think for a long time about what you meant,
but I believe I understand it. A camera just
clicks pictures of what's out there, but a
painter has to pick details from everything
she sees and decide which ones and how to
paint them. Right? If ten people paint exactly
the same scene, all ten pictures look different. I know that from art class.

It's so perfect that you used Matisse as
an example. He's my favorite artist. I have a
poster of one of his paintings hanging on my
wall (green leaves and a goldfish bowl—do
you know it?). I also have a calendar of his
paintings. When I look at them, I always
want to move right into his rooms and walk
barefoot across his carpets. I want to talk to
his beautiful women and ask them what
they're reading. Or plunk my hand in that

goldfish bowl! Can't you just *feel* it all? I
always thought, if only I could write a book
that would make people feel things, the way
I feel when I look at one of those paintings.
I love how all of his surfaces are flat. The
table under the goldfish bowl is painted
round instead of the way we're taught to
show perspective in art class—as if the whole
world were light and bright and would just
bob away if ugliness tried to touch it.

I'm so relieved you like my writing. I've
been trying to tell myself I could take it if
you didn't, but I don't think I really could.
Criticism yes, but rejection no. It's too
important to me. Lately I've been having
trouble believing in myself as a writer. I
write something and I think I like it, but
when I read it the next day it all sounds
childish. I can never please myself. Probably
I read too much. I'm always comparing
myself to "the Greats" and I never seem
good enough.

I've been reading *The Portrait of a Lady*
by Henry James. Have you ever read it?
Isabel Archer is such a wonderful character,
and James's descriptions of places and houses

send goose bumps down my spine.

I wish I could go somewhere—any-where—and see things. My father is a workaholic and won't take a vacation. This summer he's making me get a job too. He says it will be good for me to stick my nose into the real world instead of into a book. I told him I'd be happy to stick it into another country, but he just laughs. He always laughs. He doesn't have a clue. Thank goodness I read, or I might not even know that somewhere the world is full of interesting people. BUT WHERE ARE THEY? I guess in New York City, being writers and editors. And one is in Virginia.

I'm so sorry about your father. I can't imagine how it will be, having my parents grow old and die. Even though I resent them most of the time (sometimes even hate them), I want them to always be there. Weird, isn't it? And it is scary to think about how you can't control something that matters that much in your life.

Thank you again for everything. I hope I'll have another chapter soon. It's funny, when you compliment me, it makes me happy but also scared. What if I'm not as good as you think but have just been lucky so far? I hope I don't disappoint you.

Very sincerely,
Liz (which is what
my *friends* call me!)

June 2, 1995

Dear Liz,

I must confess your letter startled me. It reminded me of how especially precious beauty is to the awakening eye, something those of us who publish for the young should always keep in the forefront of our minds. You remind me of me when I was young and make me lonesome a bit for my old self. I think you will someday write the book you dream of writing. Look what you've made me feel already.

It's good to read "the Greats" but wrong to compare yourself to them. You're only just beginning. What they have to teach you is slipping in your back door and lingering in your kitchen. After it's been simmered, bits and pieces will pop up in the most surprising places. But don't consciously imitate. Just write what you have to write. You're doing very well being Liz Beech. Your skills will grow. And don't worry about living up to my expectations—I haven't imagined you, you know. Your talent is real, and you can

rely on it as long as you keep on working.
Work includes making mistakes, which you
will do, but mistakes won't cancel out past
achievements or change my opinion of you.
Don't be afraid of the process.

I have read *The Portrait of a Lady*, but
many years ago. I remember the spunky
Miss Archer—no surprise to me that you
like her. I marvel that a person your age can
master such a book. James is difficult.
You're quite a wonder. Are you planning on
college one day? Aim high. But of course
you already do.

Keep sending whatever you're ready to
send to this address. I have to sell my parents' house, and this will keep me here a
good while yet. It's curious to be out of the
New York fray—I haven't been for years—
and to be back at the scene of my early life,
dismantling it, no less. I don't quite know
what to do with all the emotions that I'm
feeling. If I were Liz Beech, I'd write a
book. Believe me, you don't have to live in
New York City to do it. In fact, I don't
know that a writer even should be in New
York City. It hasn't done much for me

except wear down my edges until I feel I'm quite without shape. Any number of people could step into my shoes at work and things would go on just the same. I'm not really needed. Isn't this an odd thing to discover in the middle of a life?

All the best,
Julia

Dear Journal,

Do I remind you of anyone? A certain professional editor, perhaps, when she was young? Or the spunky Miss Archer? My life is starting to feel so weird. It's like there's the me I am in the house and at school and then the me of my writing and letters. We all know which me *you* like the best. So do I.

Julia (yes, she asked me to call her that!) makes me feel that it really is true what I've always felt—that in some way I'm special or different and that I have a very particular, specific future ahead that I'm somehow supposed to prepare for and meet. Do you think this is snobby and egotistical? It probably is, but still it's the way I feel. Mrs. Reeves always thought this about me too, back in the days when she lived on the planet Earth and made actual eye contact with Earthlings.

I'm going to stop now and write a letter to Julia and then go study for finals—which I never have time to do since I'm always out looking for jobs. Does this fact bother my father? No, it does not. It seems to be more important to him that I work this summer than that I do well in school. Do you know where I applied for a job today?—Dunkin Donuts! I told my father it wouldn't be cost-effective since after only a week he'd have to hire a crane to lift me up out of a chair and carry me off to work. He actually smirked, which is his form of laughter, and said he guessed I had a point. He also said later that he supposed I also had a point about getting a job at a place where I might enjoy it, assuming that I could find one, since this was my first working experience. Holy cow—father-daughter communication! I almost fell out of my chair. My mother, who came in at the end of the conversation, said she wished I would work in the mall at someplace like The Limited so I could buy my clothes at a discount. Isn't it touching how well she knows me? I haven't even been to the mall since The Limited moved in there! Sometimes I think she confuses me with Kelly, her true dream child.

Well, dear Journal, I said I was going to stop writing but I guess that I forgot to, which is pretty depressing. When I first started writing in you, I thought I'd be only recording my deep philosophical thoughts about writing, but this always seems to happen—the ordinary part of me gets jealous or something and grabs the pen and just starts writing. All I can say is, apologies to both of us. (I mean you and the purer me.)

Dear Julia,

How could you say that about your job
and not being needed? I'll bet you've edited
so many beautiful books that are better
because of you. I know nobody else could
write such interesting letters or *would* write
them to a sixteen-year-old beginner.

I love it that I remind you of you when
you were young. Until now Mrs. Reeves was
the only person who believed in me. It
sounds pompous, I know, but deep down
inside I've always believed that I have some
special future—a Destiny or something—and
that I have to work to meet it. I can't say
that to anyone here because they'll call me a
snob, which most people already do. I'm not
a snob. I don't think I'm better than most
other people. Just different. And gifted, I
guess. But I didn't give myself my gifts, if
they really are there. My mother calls me
"Little Miss High and Mighty" when I say
things like this, so I never do. You and Mrs.

Reeves are the only people who've ever understood why I think of myself as a writer and why that makes me different.

I can't take too much credit for reading and liking Henry James. I didn't like him, at first. I was only reading *The Portrait of a Lady* because it's Mrs. Reeves's favorite book. The things she says about Henry James always made me want to like him, so I tried. I almost gave it up before I came to Isabel Archer. But when her sister's husband said, "Isabel's written in a foreign tongue. I can't make her out," I just stared at the words. It's how everyone around here feels about me, I know it, and there it is, so perfectly said.

I'm sure it sounds egotistical, but I've been collecting sentences about Isabel Archer that sound like me. The best one is "her imagination was by habit ridiculously active; when the door was not open it jumped out of the window." At first I just felt relieved to know that the world must hold other people like me. But then, more importantly, I began to think how wonderful it was that James could describe an imagination that "jumped out of the window" when the door was closed. What a wonderful image!

So I've begun to love Henry James, even though he can make me crazy with his long, weird sentences no one could ever unwind. And the character Pansy must be the most ridiculous sixteen-year-old ever created! I hate to think what would happen to *her* at Edgewood Heights High! (I think *I* have it rough!) Anyway, the secret to reading Henry James, I think, is to read little bits at a time. Right now I'm taking a break from *The Portrait of a Lady* so I can read some other things.

I don't know about college. I always assumed that I would go, but my parents and I have never discussed it, which is weird, I guess. My brother, Roger, is graduating this year, and he's not going, but in his case it's no surprise. He's moving to California. I guess the only thing we really plan on in this family is escape.

It must be awful to sell your parents' house if you grew up in it and had a happy childhood there. If I had a house like that, I could never let it go.

Anyway, here's Chapter Three. I hope you like it!

Sincerely,
Liz

Chapter Three

ELSPETH THE PING-PONG BALL. She bounced back to her mother's house.

"He really said it?" Her mother smacked her hand on her forehead, amazed. "He *said* he was dating Patsy?"

Elspeth nodded. "But Mom, you knew. It's not such a big surprise."

Her mother flung herself onto the sofa and wailed. The sound danced along Elspeth's spine.

"Go and pack your suitcase," her mother said when she finally recovered. "You're moving out of that house!"

Elspeth went. Out of the frying pan into the fire. So that's what that expression meant.

At her father's she filled her suitcase with books. If only she owned enough, she would pile them around her like a fort.

"Where do you think you're going?" her father said when she'd bumped the suitcase down the stairs and into the kitchen.

Elspeth sighed. "I'm moving to Mom's. She told me to."

Her father's jaw dropped. "The hell you are!" He banged a hand on the table and stood up. "Take that suitcase back upstairs!"

Elspeth turned around and slid the suitcase back through the doorway. Behind her the outside door slammed as her father headed for her mother's.

At the foot of the stairs she sat down on a step to wait. There was no way she was going to lug this thing back upstairs until the argument was over. She should just take her suitcase and run (or slide!) to the nearest exit and keep on going. Her parents would be so busy arguing about where she should live, they wouldn't notice she was gone.

Yes. That was what she'd do. But she couldn't move. Suddenly, as she sat there, a great, lonely feeling of yearning came over her. A yearning to be living in some other generation, when parents acted like grown-ups and knew what to do, or to be already in the future, when she would be grown up herself and know what to do. A yearning to live anywhere, in any time, except here and now.

"All right," her father said when he came back. "Go."

"Go?" He was giving her up, just like that?

"If you want to be with that woman, go on and go." His face was splotchy with anger. "But you'd better watch out—it's enough that you look like your mother, you don't want to act like her too."

"Dad, I *don't* want to be with her. I never said that, once. She *ordered* me to go!" Not that she wanted to be here either. "And I *don't* look like my mother! Not one bit!"

But he wasn't listening. He never listened. Elspeth dragged her suitcase back through the kitchen and across the yard.

"Yes!" her mother said when Elspeth came through the door. She gave a thumbs-up-for-victory sign, her eyes bright.

"I told him I'd sue him!" her mother said. "I told the rat I'd take him to court for corrupting an innocent minor!"

Elspeth sat on top of her suitcase. Where did the people live who wrote beautiful books? she wondered. Was there one particular place on earth where grown-ups thought about poetry and beauty? And why didn't she live there? She closed her eyes. She imagined that her suitcase was a magic carpet that could take her far away to that other, better place.

"What are you doing, Elspeth?" her mother asked. "Why are you sitting like that?"

Elspeth was very still on top of her suitcase, her legs and arms folded Indian style. "I'm taking a magic suitcase ride." She didn't open her eyes. She couldn't bear to see that the scenery hadn't changed.

Dear Journal,

If only there *were* a magic suitcase and I could take a ride. I'm so sick of school and home and life in general. Mrs. Reeves has turned into a major disappointment. She's the one who made me write to an editor in the first place, but does she ever ask me about my writing or about what Julia has to say? No, she doesn't. And I don't bother to tell her either. She has this funny faraway look in her eyes lately, as if only her body is here. Other than to say that, I don't know how to explain her.

I applied for a job today in a nearby day-care center. In the summer it becomes a sort of day camp for kids of all ages. I'd help with crafts and games if I got the job. So far it's the best one I've applied for. I wanted to apply at Encore or Barnes & Noble but can't figure out how I would get there since there's no one reliable to drive me every day. Roger (who's been driving my mother's car!) will be gone, and my mother's work schedule is so erratic (like her old car and her personality and her interest in motherhood in general) that I could never depend on her.

I'm going to quit writing in you and go start a new chapter. I've got my character Elspeth living with her mother, which should be good for a few laughs. I have to say one thing about *my* mother—she's totally crazy and useless as a mother but she can be pretty funny sometimes. I can see how living with my passive and boring father might have driven her over the edge. Sometimes I wish I could meet the person she was before she got married and see if I like her. (And figure out why she married my father!)

June 17, 1995

Dear Liz,

I've just read your excellent Chapter
Three. Your story is growing more and more
lively. I can't help wondering how much of it
is drawn from life, but I'm not going to ask
because it's none of my business and truly
not relevant either. It's just the editor in me,
ever curious to understand how imagination
shapes the raw material of life. Anyway, congratulations and keep on going.

Yes, it's hard to sell a house in which
you've been happy. I had a blessed, wonderful childhood with parents who loved and
encouraged me at every turn. They were
older when I was born and had long since
given up hope of having children, when I
came along and surprised them. I was lucky
and always knew it. Even so, the time came
when I longed for escape, as every young
person does, and my parents let me go.

Now I'm letting them go. But not easily.
In truth, I want everything back. I find I
can't throw away any of their things as I sort

through drawers and closets. Honestly, are people ever not yearning for where they've been or where they're going? A very fine use you made of the word "yearning" in your story, by the way. It's one of those truly evocative words.

I hope you will consider college. Discuss it with your parents. I should think you'd need to begin looking at schools fairly soon. But college isn't the only way, of course, and it's not my place to say what's right for you. You'll blossom wherever you go. It's the benefit of having an imagination that can jump through windows!

It's interesting, what you said about feeling a sense of destiny. I used to feel that way too—that I was intended for something special. I wonder if everyone privately feels the very same thing. And why not? We are all, after all, unique, and each of us has a mission. If anyone has a purpose, then I guess all of us do.

But in my heart of hearts I believe that some are special. I think you are. And maybe I was. But I never marched forward to meet my destiny with the bold, sure stride you seem to possess. How curious that you've come along at this point in my life, when I'm thrown back to my own youth and am remembering. And how curious that I tell you such things. I'm behaving quite unprofessionally. Why don't I care?

Keep those chapters coming.

Affectionately,
Julia

Dear Journal of a Person with a Bold, Sure Stride,

Stop laughing. If an editor (especially an editor who signs her letters "Affectionately"!) says it, then maybe it's true. I *am* trying to march forward to meet my destiny. Just because my stride doesn't *feel* bold and sure, it doesn't mean I'm not moving, does it?

Okay, yes, maybe Julia's behavior is unprofessional and yes, maybe I do wish she'd care about that just a little. I can't help thinking, here I have an editor who's a real editor interested in my writing, and she suddenly decides to stop acting like an editor. She's not even going to an office! So who, exactly, *is* she then, at least to me? But I think all of her weird behavior is because of her parents' being old and dying and her having to be in Virginia, and you can't really blame her for that. Plus the things she writes are so truthful and beautiful and interesting, why would I ever want her to stop? Reading her letters is like reading Henry James and suddenly seeing that another world IS really out there. I just have to be mature and accept that she's writing to me as a grown-up or a friend (or maybe as a journal!) and learn from the things she says.

I'm loving my Chapter Four. It's really pretty funny and has been so much fun to write. This amazing thing's started happening—Elspeth now thinks for herself, apart from me. I don't know how to explain this since, of course, whatever she thinks is really coming from me. All I can say is she is much bolder and funnier and brighter than I have ever been. I'm sort of jealous of her! I *cannot* explain that!

Dear Julia,

Thank you so much! I'm glad you liked
my chapter. It is all fiction, but it's interesting how it's also not. I mean my mother
really has used me to spy on my father a
million times. When I was younger (before I
knew there was nothing at all to find out
about my boring father), I used to worry that
I'd discover something awful and have to tell
her about it. My father never dated my
mother's best friend, but he used to talk to
her, and once they went for a really long
walk and it worried me a lot. It was exciting
and scary, pulling up that old fear and using
it for my book.

Also, in real life my father and mother do
"talk" to each other, if you can call it that.
My mother shouts and my father sulks and
then eventually he "guides" her to her side of
the house and locks her out of ours. I think
they enjoy it, or why wouldn't they move?
They used to say they shared this house "for

the kids' sakes." Then they said they couldn't afford separate quarters. None of that's true anymore. They're just weird. My book is about people who are weird—who both love and hate each other. My parents, but not my parents too.

I feel so sorry for you, having to sort through drawers and all your parents' things. Couldn't you just keep the house? Maybe someday you'll live there again. If you ever have time, describe the house to me.

It's interesting what you say about people always yearning (I love that word too). I know exactly what you mean. I've been yearning my whole life to be grown up, but only last week I was looking at my old dollhouse and remembering exactly how it felt to love all those little rooms. All of a sudden I wanted to be small again. I felt a really deep ache, down inside myself. And that's yearning, right?

Maybe only certain people can feel it. Do you think? I mean my mother wants to find a man and have a perfect marriage, but she doesn't want it in a *yearning* sort of way. She wants it in a go-out-and-look-for-the-guy-then-trap-him sort of way, if you know what I mean.

Here's Chapter Four. If you don't like it, I have five other versions. I keep changing my mind about what should come next. And something strange is starting to happen— Elspeth is suddenly doing all these things I'd never do (and maybe don't even want to!), but I still feel like I know and understand her. It's sort of a bonus—like there get to be two of me!

Affectionately to you,
too—
Liz

P.S. I'll be working in a day-care center this summer, which is okay I guess. Better than Burger King, but not as good as a bookstore. Whether I do or don't go to college, my goal is to one day run a bookstore (and write too, of course).

Chapter Four

IN THE NEXT FEW WEEKS, Elspeth's mother went back and forth from being sad to being angry, from being angry to wanting revenge, then back again to sad. She was a loose live wire.

It was only a matter of time, of course, before she lost her job. Who needed a loose live wire working at a receptionist's desk? She'd probably cried one week away, right there in the lobby. Elspeth could picture it: "Is Mr. Segal in?" someone would ask. "Who cares?" her mother would sob.

In a perverse sort of way, losing her job made her mother happy. It was more time she could spend spying and fuming and crying and one more thing she could blame on Elspeth's father.

"He takes everything I have!" her mother shouted. "He took you! He took Patsy! Now he took my job!"

Elspeth rolled her eyes and buried her

head in a book. Still, she had to admit that the sight of Patsy going in and out of her father's house was driving *her* wild too. The last time she'd gone to collect her belongings, Patsy's clothes had been hanging in Elspeth's closet while Elspeth's were in piles on the bed—and not neat piles, either.

Impulsively, Elspeth had emptied all the little pebbles from her old terrarium into Patsy's shoes lined up in the closet. Then she'd rushed home in alarm and stared in the mirror. How much *did* she look like her mother? Not much, she reassured herself. Maybe their smiles were the same.

"Are you letting your mother into my house?" her father asked the next day. He'd rushed out to catch her as she left for school.

"Of course not!" Elspeth opened her eyes wide and smiled innocently, the way her mother did when she wanted to drive someone crazy. It was a subtle and creative form of punishment, she thought, to have her father thinking there might soon be two loose live wires flipping around the neighborhood and no one to blame but himself. As long as *she* knew the truth—that she was nothing at all like her mother.

One afternoon her father and Patsy walked past the house holding hands. Looking happy! Elspeth couldn't believe it. Luckily, her mother wasn't near any windows. Jerks, she thought. Suddenly she was glad her mother was crazy and vindictive and more angry now than sad. She was even glad she'd begun spending most of her time thinking up creative forms of torture. Go for it, Mom!

Elspeth had never fully appreciated how creative her mother was, either. In Elspeth's humble opinion, her cat food idea bordered on genius. Every afternoon her mother sprinkled a ring of dry food around her father's house, and within minutes the army of strays that lived in the field out back would appear and eat up the evidence. Then they'd stay, of course, having been invited: a little welcoming committee for the cat-hater Patsy. Patsy would stand in the driveway looking at them like they were lions and then yell and stomp and go charging up the stairs.

"Such a lovely smell there is over there now," Elspeth's mother reflected one afternoon as they watched Patsy slam through the door. Behind her a male cat lifted its tail and sprayed at the steps. Elspeth and her mother smiled at each other.

This was some form of genius, Elspeth thought again. Her mother had mastered a twisted kind of art form.

"You're sort of an artist, Mom," she said when they'd gone back to the kitchen to find some supper.

"Why thank you, dear." Her mother smiled. But the smile was disturbingly familiar. Elspeth had seen it recently in the mirror.

"I think you should stop now, though," she added hastily. "It's time to get on with your life." She sounded like a bad actor in a corny movie, even to herself. But someone in the house had to pretend to be an adult, and it was not going to be her mother.

"Stop what?" Her mother smeared peanut butter across several slices of bread and cut a banana onto the top of it all. She handed a slice to Elspeth.

Elspeth sighed and ate. She supposed there was no stopping an artist from doing what an artist had to do. Anyway, what could she say with her mouth stuck shut?

Dear Journal of a Completely Exhausted
Person,

I started work today, and I am so tired I
cannot speak. I work with the littlest kids,
who are cute and very funny (one of them
can't say "Liz" so he calls me "Dizzy"!) but
also exhausting. I can tell that I'm not going
to feel much like writing when I get home.
This is depressing, because I'd hoped to use
this summer to finish my book for Julia.

Oh well, at least I like my job. I could be
tired from working at Burger King.

7/10/95

Dear Journal of a Person Who's Now *Used*
to Being Exhausted,

—in fact it's even sort of fun. It makes
me wacko and I bond with all the kids. The
bad news is, I've done no writing.

The other bad news is my mother. One
of the doctors she cleans for is closing down

his office, which means that at the moment my mother has extra time on her hands but a little less money, and if she can't shop, what can-n-n-n she do?? She'll now be HOME the two nights a week she used to spend cleaning his office. With Roger gone, there's no way she's going to stay on her side of the house alone. Journal, what if she makes me go stay with her? I sense disaster coming. This morning I was lying in bed trying to make myself get up when suddenly I had this bizarre fantasy that the things I wrote in my novel might all really happen to me. This was only a fantasy, right?—*not* ESP?!?

Dear Liz,

I've been laughing all day. Chapter Four is terrific.

I'm glad to know you find writing fun. It certainly shows. I've had writers tell me how much they hate to write, and I wonder why they do it.

Elspeth is taking off on her own because you've given her life. She's very well imagined. Lucky you, Liz, to have your wonderful gift. It seems to me that the point of writing is to experience what you've expressed, the thrill of living lives other than your own. It's also the point of reading, don't you think?

Thanks for explaining a little how you've turned life into fiction. It fascinates me, and not for any nosy reason. I find it exciting the way your imagination pulled up that old fear and put it to use. No wonder it was scary— the artist in you was at work. Most of us keep the little guy (or woman!) chained to the floor so he can't do any mischief.

It's a very fine point you make about only some people being yearners. Of course, you're right. True yearning (as opposed to the general "I wish I had what you have" type) is an imaginative act, isn't it? The more you can imagine yourself back into yesterday or ahead into tomorrow, the more susceptible you are to yearning for it. I can't decide if this is a character flaw or a gift. A little less yearning would get me further along in the here and now, that's for sure. On the other hand, it's what an artist draws on, I think, this sense of our yesterdays and our tomorrows all mixed up with today and what-might-have-been to create a work of art. It could almost serve as a measuring stick for art: who best has captured the yearnings? Interesting. But those of us who aren't artists, where do our yearnings go if we have them? Perhaps into nervous break-downs. Scary thought, I must say.

Anyway, thanks to all those yearnings, memories pop out of every drawer and I don't get far in my sorting. I've now taken an official extended leave of absence from Springtime, but unfortunately I've left a number of "important" projects half done in New York and my phone keeps ringing. I had to fly up there twice last month for meetings. I wish I could turn off the outside world for this one little while and just deal with what's at hand. From down here New York looks pretty silly—everyone running around pretending that what they're doing matters, when so often it doesn't.

Lately it seems as if all we're doing at Springtime is working to make money for a few people at the top and, in the process, costing the world its trees. Do the people who're making this money worry about *what* we're publishing or whether it's any good or if the world really needs it? Not lately they don't. ALL of my proposals have been rejected this year because of marketing considerations. They were good and worthy proposals that might have been worth the trees. This sounds cynical, I know, but it's simply the truth and a scary truth at that. When you've given your life to a job, you need it to give something back—to have a modicum of meaning. Anyway, this is all by way of explanation for why I don't want to rush back to New York when I have real concerns down here.

My parents' house is nothing grand. It's big and old in a drooping part of the city, but it has some lovely features. There's a deep front porch with a wooden swing and lots of trees in the yard. Southern trees— magnolias, and pecans and damsons. When I was little, I used to climb the damson trees and sell the fruit to the neighbors. My mother made damson pies (I let her have them for free). There's also wisteria draped across the porch. What a nuisance, but also what a joy when it's out in full force. New owners will cut it all down to save the sagging eaves.

Believe me, I've considered keeping the house, but to what end? My life is now in New York. I'd still have to clean out the drawers in order to rent the house to strangers. The thought of a stranger's belongings arranged in my mother's drawers is an image too awful to bear.

My poor father gets worse and worse. I think he just doesn't want to live without my mother. Thank goodness he isn't well enough to know that I'm selling the house. It would break his poor old heart.

But someone young and lively doesn't want to hear all this middle-age drudgery stuff. Forgive me. And keep the chapters coming!

With affection,
Julia

Dear Julia,

Your letter must be the most beautiful
one ever written. I can't believe it was written to *me*. I've read it a hundred times. I
love your image of everyone's little personal
artist, chained to the floor! And it's so interesting, what you say about yearning. I even
love hearing the "middle-age drudgery
stuff," though I'm very sorry it's sad. It
helps me know you better. To me it's always
interesting when someone tells you about
things that are real and important to them.
Really, almost no one ever does. Have you
noticed? I'm flattered you'd tell me. It seems
like a miracle.

I don't know how you can say you're not
an artist, because you are. The way you
describe your parents' house is just so perfect I can almost see it. And adding the part
about climbing the damson trees does just
what you said an artist should—captures a
yearning! I love the way you think and the
way you write and wish I could be so perfect.

117

Have you ever written fiction? I know you
could. I can't believe they'd turn down your
proposals at your publishing house. There
must be some major brain-deads working
at "the top." Maybe you should work at a
different place.

It doesn't seem fair of me to send you
chapters when you need peace from the outside world, but I will if you want me to—
hopefully soon. It's been hard writing lately.
I'm so tired after working in the day-care
center that the words just blur. If you
weren't out there waiting, I might not ever
do it, but since you are, I've been making
myself write at least an hour every night,
and I'm always glad when I do it.
Afterwards, if I like what I've written, I say,
"Thank you, Julia!" then drop into bed.

Love,
Liz

Dear Journal,

Tonight it happened. My mother came
over in a rage (mostly because she'd been
home alone all day) and demanded that she
and my father "share" me! Really, that was
the word she used—like I was some kind of
a toy my father had been allowed to play
with too often. They argued for a while
about "the terms of the arrangement" and
"what the papers say" before I jumped in
and pointed out that I was now sixteen and
nobody's property and could live wherever I
wanted and spend my time however I liked
and that they should both just shut up about
it. They looked at me like they'd forgotten
that I was there and couldn't remember why
it was any of my business. At which point
I realized they weren't even fighting about
me. Not really. Everything suddenly seemed
so useless and stupid that I started to cry
and stormed off to my bedroom. Things
have been quiet the rest of the night. I've
tried to work on my chapter, but I just can't.
I want to be writing about beauty, and I'm

writing about THEM and they are not even worth it.

Then I had an even more awful thought—what if what Julia says about Springtime Press is true at all publishing houses? Dear Journal, if publishers don't care about beauty, then who ever will? And how will the people who do care ever find each other?

Dear Liz,

Believe me, I am far from perfect, but I'm touched you think so and I am glad that my letter meant so much to you. Yours all mean a great deal to me. You're right. Few people *do* tell you things that are real and important, especially when you're my age and in the world of business. Telling the truth just slows things down.

I did once harbor a notion that I could write fiction, but I never did it. I let myself be moved from college into career and along the busywork track as if life were on automatic. At your young age you've climbed onto a bigger creative limb than I ever have in my forty-three years.

Please believe me: you're not the outside world I'd like to avoid. Don't hesitate whenever you want to write me. I'm curiously alone down here, since I have no relatives to speak of and my high school friends have long since moved away. I'm discovering something else, too. My friends in New York

all belong to my business world, and now
that I'm away from them, they seem less
essential to my life than I'd supposed. I'm a
very narrow person in my middle age. I like
remembering the younger me I'm encounter-
ing through your letters.

So send your chapters! And keep the letters coming.

Love,
Julia

Dear Liz,

I seem to be feeling alarmingly lonesome and confess to wishing you'd write. Are things all right with you there? I know you're busy trying to write after work and letters are time-consuming.

I've begun wondering if I should go back to work myself and let this house just wait. It's hard being inside it all the time with no distractions. Going back to New York of course would merely be postponing the inevitable, so I've had the notion of looking for work down here—maybe applying at Hollins College or Roanoke Community for some sort of teaching position. Yesterday I actually left the house to do it, but then it all suddenly seemed absurd. How can I be applying for work? I asked myself. I don't live here. And I have other commitments. I thought, Julia, what are you *doing*? It's as if I forgot who I was. But then again, who am I?

Anyway, how's your writing coming? I'd love a new chapter. Wouldn't it be nice to someday finally meet?

Love,
Julia

Dear Journal,

I'm sorry I haven't written. I've been
using my pathetic writing energy (lately
twenty minutes a night and that's on a good
night) to work on a chapter for Julia. I
haven't been writing to her, dear Journal,
either, and now she's sent me the weirdest
letter saying how she's lonesome and hopes
that we'll one day meet. I mean it is really
flattering, but it's sort of scary too. Why
does she need a letter from me, when she's
an adult professional and I'm a sixteen-year-
old high school person whom she's never
met?

On the other hand, we're common spir-
its, and when you're lonely and going
through hard times like Julia is—like *both* of
us are—that can really be important. The other
day I heard someone on TV say that there
were these ancient peoples (or maybe
Indians? I was unfortunately only half listening) who believed that in the beginning of
time we all belonged to tribes but that our
tribes had somehow gotten scattered. When

we meet a person and feel an instant connection, it means we're meeting someone from our tribe, and we're supposed to strive to hold on to and know that person forever. This so perfectly explains how I feel about living in my neighborhood in New Jersey—there's nobody here from my tribe. And I guess it's how Julia feels about working in a place where nobody respects what she values. So her letter isn't that weird at all. But now I'm too tired to answer it. Not to mention that trouble seems to be brewing out in the hallway. My mother, of course.

Dear Julia,

Your letter sounded so sad. I'm sorry I
haven't written or sent my chapter sooner,
it's just that there hasn't been one to send
you. Lately I've been having trouble separat-
ing Elspeth's parents from my own when I
write, and it makes me not want to bother.
Maybe it's because it's summer and our
house isn't air conditioned so people's tem-
pers are over the top, but my parents seem
worse than ever. Last night my mother started
a *food fight*, across the center hall. My father
locked our door and just sat there while
tomatoes and eggs splatted the walls. I hate
him when he does that—just goes dumb and
blank when he should be fighting back. Or
at least taking control. Isn't he supposed to
be a grown-up? It makes my mother go
twice as crazy when he doesn't respond in
some way. It's worse than when he fights.

Anyway, I'm sick of adults who act like
children, and writing about them isn't much
fun. I feel like writing a fairy tale or a really

beautiful poem. I just want to put beauty into the world. But I can't. I don't feel any beauty inside me at the moment. This is very scary.

It's funny how when you wrote you seemed to be feeling friendless, because right now I am too. My best friend, Kelly, and her sister, Shana, are in Maine with their dad for the month of August. Every year, since we were little, he's taken them there and they've invited me to go. And every year my father says no. It's sort of become a joke. This year they didn't even ask me. I know they figured they shouldn't since I have a job and also Shana's husband will be there for part of the time. But still, it really hurt me.

Anyway, here's my latest chapter. I'm not too happy with it. It's sort of a downer, like me. Sorry. And yes, it would be great to meet you. I don't know what to say about your idea of getting a job at a college in Roanoke. You're so wonderful as an editor, and some selfish part of me wants you to always be one. But you'd be a wonderful teacher, too. I do know what you mean about suddenly forgetting who you are. I've done that often lately—in fact, it can feel like a state of being!

I hope things are better for you soon.

Love,
Liz

Chapter Five

FOR A WHILE ELSPETH tried to pretend that
the war going on was funny. Sometimes it
was, too. Like when her father was trimming
the hedges with his electric clippers and, in a
burst of inspiration, trimmed the heads off her
mother's tulips. There they stood in their silly
little rows, being mini decapitations. Amusing.
And the cats still came every day.

But things got worse. When Elspeth heard
her mother on the phone with Patsy's boss,
she knew things had gone too far. "She has a
troublesome, contagious disease," she heard her
mother saying. "*I* wouldn't want her around."

That did it. Elspeth had to tell her father.

"Mom's causing Patsy problems," she
told him that weekend. With rare luck both
her mother and Patsy had gone out at the
same time. She'd paused to enjoy a temporary
fantasy that they were at the movies together
the way they used to be on Saturday after-
noons.

"Tell me something I don't already know," her father answered. He was washing the dishes. *(Washing the dishes?)* "Your mother is a nut case. I hate your living over there."

Elspeth sighed. "Well, she wasn't—not before." Or had she been? Elspeth really couldn't remember.

Her father rolled his eyes.

"She *wasn't!* She's had a hard life, you know!" And this was true—a life caused by Elspeth's father, who had never washed the dishes for her mother. Not once! She was almost sorry that she'd come. Then she remembered the phone call. Okay, so her mother *was* a nut case.

"Has Patsy had trouble at work?" she forced herself to ask.

Her father stopped washing and looked up in surprise. "Why?" he said. "What do you know?"

Elspeth told him about the phone call. His face turned red. "You can't tell her I told you!" she rushed to say.

"I most certainly can," he replied softly. He narrowed his eyes. "This time she's gone too far."

"Dad! Don't tell her I told you. I just wanted—Patsy—to know. I think Mom did it because she lost *her* job."

"Your mother lost her job?" Her father frowned. And on what planet had he been living? Elspeth wondered. "What are you doing for money?"

Elspeth shrugged.

"Are you eating, or what?"

Elspeth shrugged again. They'd never really eaten. Not in the meal sense of the word. Peanut butter. Cheerios. If her mother bought fruit and vegetables, it was to throw at her father's house. They ate when Elspeth cooked.

"Here." Her father reached into his pocket and pulled out a twenty-dollar bill. "You keep an eye on your mother. Tell me everything she does."

Elspeth didn't touch the money.

"What do they do over there?" her mother asked. She'd come home unexpectedly and seen Elspeth leaving her father's. "Are Patsy's clothes in the closet? Does Patsy cook? Has she hung her own pictures up?" Her eyes had a funny, shiny look.

"I don't know, Mom," Elspeth said. "I didn't look around." She didn't mention the dishes.

"You didn't look around?" Her mother looked amazed. "Then what did you go there for?"

Elspeth thought this over. "For the pleasure of seeing them squirm," she lied. It was a little present to her mother.

And her mother looked pleased. "Did they?" she asked.

Elspeth shrugged. "Patsy wasn't there."

"Really?" Her mother's eyebrows knit together. "Huh. I wonder where she was."

"And I wonder if we'll ever eat in this house," Elspeth said, partly to change the subject and partly because her stomach had started growling.

"Oh." Her mother looked vaguely towards the kitchen. "Go see. I think there's some peanut butter. Or was."

There was peanut butter. But no jelly or bread. Elspeth dug her finger deep into the jar and licked it off. She should have taken the money from her father. Next time she would.

Well, Dear Journal,

Julia wrote and begged for a letter and chapter, and then when I sent one she didn't answer. Now *I* feel like writing a begging letter. Sometimes it just seems too appropriate that the kids at the center have started calling me "Dizzy"! On Friday I let them all spin me around, and for one second, after I stopped being dizzy, the world seemed perfectly clear and straight. Journal, I loved that second.

Dear Liz,

Thank you for your letter and chapter. I'm sorry to hear you've been depressed also; however, it didn't hurt your writing, if that's any consolation. In fact, you've drawn on it very nicely. It makes sense that Elspeth would be feeling just such a depression herself.

I confess to being a little startled by your mother's food fight. You seldom mention her in your letters. What's she like? The food fight offers a clue, I guess. I must say, this "same house" arrangement your parents have doesn't seem very healthy to me— though it would, of course, if it worked!

I'm sorry too about Kelly's not inviting you. My guess is that, as you say, she just assumed you couldn't go. Maybe things will be better when you're both back at school. Or maybe you're simply outgrowing each other. It seems we could both use a few new friends. Sometimes I think I simply don't try hard enough to find them. Friends seldom just up and land on your doorstep (although, lucky for me, *you* did).

No, I'm not going to look for work. How foolish of me to mention it. I'm here in the house, doing my duty, and then spending time with my poor old father, who seems curiously resigned to his nursing home. Which makes me both sad and happy.

Write to me when you can.

Love,
Julia

Dear Journal,

Say this isn't happening. The one thing besides writing that's made life liveable is the fact that I like school. Well, guess what?— this year I don't. Mrs. Reeves DID NOT COME BACK. It turns out she's having a baby. Lame—you can teach and still have babies. So. I hate all of my courses. I hate all of my teachers. I hate Kelly, who dyed her hair blond this summer and fell "in love" with some guy in Maine. This I won't even discuss. Yes, I could use new friends, as Julia suggested, and no, I suppose they won't just up and land on my doorstep. But where do I go to look for them? I've known every kid in my school since an eon before my birth, and while plenty of them might be nice, we never have interests in common. Or if we do, the kids I like don't like me back. Which has been true since kindergarten.

Journal, how will I get through this year?

September 8, 1995

Dear Liz,

I'm off to New York for a supposedly
brief stint but wanted to let you know.

I'm a little worried not to have heard
from you since you sent me your last chapter. Are things all right? I hope you're not
still depressed. No doubt my own rumblings
of self-pity didn't help you a bit. Chin up,
Liz. Things will get better for both of us.
I'm trying to trust in that.

Love,

J.

September 14, 1995

Dear Julia,

Maybe things will get better, but at the moment it's hard to believe. School has started, and this year I hate it too. Mrs. Reeves, my English teacher for the last two years (remember her?), didn't come back. She left to have a baby. I'm really surprised. Not that she had a baby, but that she decided not to come back. She was such a wonderful teacher. She told me it was her dream, for her whole life, to be a teacher. So she teaches two years and quits! Does that make sense?

She was supposed to teach creative writing, but now they've canceled the course. Instead, I'm in Honors English with *Mr. Gerard P. Grisham* (need I say more?). This man lectures and points his finger and spins around fast, trying to embarrass someone. What a jerk. He's also big on grammar. Fine, but we learned it in middle school. It's a waste. In fact, I hate all of my teachers this year.

Sometimes I think I *should* go to college, because maybe there I'd have real teachers and I'd finally learn something worth knowing. And maybe I'd make friends, like you said we need to do. People at college would be much more interesting. Other times I think it would just be more of the same.

In answer to your questions about my mother—I guess I don't talk about her much because I don't see her much. She cleans for people, mostly doctors' offices, so she's out a lot at night and on weekends when I'm at home. My mother isn't a bad person, I guess, but we're so different. (Even our smiles!) There's nothing we can ever share or agree on. She loves me in a warped sort of way, but I disappoint her because I'm not popular and don't think about boys and clothes and hairdos. So far I haven't met the boy or hairdo worth thinking about! She desires a cheerleader type. She would be the perfect Mother of Kelly. Or at least Kelly would be the perfect daughter for her.

I hope things *are* better for you. Are you back in Virginia again or still in New York and where should I send my letters? I'll send this one to Virginia since you didn't tell me not to.

Love,
Liz

September 19, 1995

Dear Liz,

Yes, I'm back in Virginia again, so send things to me here. I'm sorry that school is bad. There's always a Mr. Grisham. I had one myself (mine was a Mrs.), but to have only teachers you hate is a sad state of affairs. All the more reason to keep on writing, both stories and letters. I suspect Mr. Grisham will fast become your ally when he learns of your talent.

I hope you do go to college, Liz, if for no other reason than it's four more years of time to grow before the world steps in to narrow you down. And you would make new friends. On the other hand, I suspect you'd do fine without it. Your star is lit and you'll surely follow. You need someone to advise you. Doesn't your school have a guidance counselor?

No, things aren't better here either. In fact, my father seems to have had a stroke, on top of everything else. I can hardly bear to leave him when I visit. He brightens when I come into the room and hangs his head when I go, so I know that he's aware. It's pathetic but very touching. Draining, too.

Needless to say, I get nowhere cleaning out the house, but I'm feeling less pressure to do so, as I've sublet my New York apartment through the spring. When I was up there last week, a copyeditor was lamenting her long commute, and on the spur of the moment I offered her the place. It seemed silly to have it sitting there empty most of the time, and I can stay in a hotel when I have to be in New York. On the way back to Virginia, though, it struck me that I'd rented away my home! So I'm not going to rush to sell this one. Anyway, I'm certain to be here awhile. There's no way I can leave my father.

I'm not exactly the person to cheer you, am I? Perhaps I shouldn't try. Sometimes life is simply sad and hard and what's the point of denying it? When I feel like crying, I go ahead and cry. Truth be told, I don't admire stoics, though I seem to have been

one all these years. Write when you can, Liz.
Your letters are part of what keeps me
going.

Love,
Julia

Dear Journal,

I've been trying to write to Julia to tell her I'm sorry her father had a stroke. My letters are "part of what keeps her going" (!), but I just can't write one. I don't even know why, except that I feel really empty inside.

Mr. Grisham has me paralyzed, that's all I can think. I try to write something or describe how I feel, but the words just don't come out. I feel them building up inside me, but they *do not come out*, even the boring stuff we have to do in class. I'm all panicky when I try.

Also, Julia sounds so sad. I can't really deal with that. I don't know how to deal with that. But I have to. Julia's my friend.

I'm going to go write to her now. I'll just make myself do it.

September 23, 1995

Dear Julia,

It's so awful that your father had a
stroke. It sounds so sad. I can't believe you
have time to think about me when you're
busy with him, but I'm glad you do.

I know my problems are nothing compared to the life-and-death ones you're having, but they're not getting better. I HATE
Mr. Grisham. He assigned us all of these
essays we had to write in class. On the first
one he wrote I was a careless, sloppy writer
who tried to think too fast. Then he stood
behind me and watched me write the next
one. Of course I couldn't with old Eagle
Eyes watching, so he accused me of
not trying. He said I had an "attitude"!
Every day he finds something to criticize.
He likes criticizing me, I can see it in his
eyes. I think he's an evil man. And he
makes me doubt my writing, which is making me doubt ME.

I guess it's no surprise that I don't have
a chapter to send you. Anyway, it would

just take your time when you should be
worrying about your father. Do you think
he can ever get better? I hate that there are
things that are awful and sad that can't
ever be changed. I don't know about stoics.
My dictionary says a stoic is someone who
"appears to or claims to be indifferent to
pleasure or pain." That sounds pretty dishonest, but it might be useful at times (like
in Mr. Grisham's class!). I'd rather be real
though, like you say, and cry when I feel
like crying, even if sometimes it makes me
feel worse.

Love,
Liz

September 27, 1995

Dear Liz,

Heavens, your Mr. Grisham sounds like a horror. Why don't you drop his class? Some things that are awful and sad *can* be changed.

But no, my father won't ever get better. And you're right, it's shocking to have to acknowledge that some things are simply final. I'm having the queerest experiences, Liz. Sometimes I completely forget my life since childhood. I'll think I'm a kid again and expect to find my mother in the kitchen, and then such a bolt shoots through me when I have to remember the truth. Needless to say, people aren't pleased with me in New York, where my grown-up self still works, at least in theory. And you're exactly right about stoics. They're dishonest. And life denying.

Please talk to your guidance counselor—about Mr. Grisham and about your plans for college. If you look toward your future, you'll see that it's very bright. Doing something to plan it should help lift you out of your slump. And good heavens, don't let Mr. Grisham stop invincible Elspeth. Write the next chapter.

Love,
Julia

Dear Julia,

Thank you for your advice. I guess I
could drop Mr. Grisham, but it would mean
dropping Honors English, and that's hard
for me to do. I'm proud of being in Honors,
and it's good to have it on my transcript if I
decide to go to college. Also, dropping
would mean Mr. Grisham had somehow
won, and the thought really annoys me.

We have guidance counselors, but I've
never talked to mine. I guess I will if you
think I should. It might help since I don't
have friends to really talk to. Kelly doesn't
care anymore. She's friends with these other
girls—big-haired types, if you know what I
mean. When I don't approve of the things
they do, Kelly calls me a snob. I guess I am
a snob, since I *don't* approve. Lately I've
been going to her sister Shana's apartment
while Kelly goes out with her friends. How
lame is that? Shana's nice, but I know I bug
her if I stay too long, so after a while I go
home. (Yes, Shana is the "Sammy" of my

original first chapter and the apartment is *that* apartment.)

Right now it's hard to believe in my future. Everywhere I look, I see grown-ups who are unhappy. Why should I think things will be different for me? It's really scary to be feeling like this and then to be reading along in *The Portrait of a Lady* and come to the shocker—Isabel marries that creep Osmond?? I hate Henry James! It's all so sudden: Isabel's soaring along like a bird and then—*ping!*—James shoots her out of the sky. Why? What does he mean? That nobody's dreams can come true? Was she a fool for aiming so high or a fool for falling so low? I keep reading and reading, thinking I'll understand, but it only gets worse.

Why am I writing this awful letter? I guess so I won't feel alone. Selfish, I know. I'm not used to being depressed, even when I'm unhappy. I'm like Isabel when James says that, for her, suffering "was an active condition; it was not a chill, a stupor, a despair; it was a passion of thought, of speculation, of response to every pressure." And that's how I've always felt, like I could fight

things and make them better. Lately I don't
even care. I'm only very sad. I CANNOT
write a chapter and don't even want to.

I shouldn't send this letter, but I'm going
to stop and mail it right now because it's
made me feel much better and I'll feel even
better if I mail it. A million apologies with it!

Sincerely,
Liz

Dear Julia,

Wow! It was so weird to hear your voice. It didn't match the voice in your letters, but then that one is in my head! Now I wonder what you look like. I have a sort of picture, and based on what? Nothing real. Your voice. My imagination does more than jump out of windows, I guess.

It was unbelievably nice of you to call. I'm sorry my letter alarmed you. Selfishly speaking, I'm glad it did, because your phone call was one of the nicest things that ever happened to me. Thank you. But please don't worry. Your being depressed didn't make me worse. I'm glad you tell me about your feelings. If you didn't, I'd be hurt.

My father wanted to know who you were and I told him the basics—that you were an editor at Springtime Press and that you were helping me with a book. He thought this over for about a century and then never said a word. Didn't ask any questions about my writing or what you thought.

He does keep looking at me kind of funny. I can't describe it, except to say that it's odd. So is he impressed or not? How can you ever know with my father?

I took your advice and today I talked to my guidance counselor. She agreed with you about dropping Mr. Grisham, even if it means dropping out of Honors. I've decided I really don't care. I won't learn anything from him, so what's the point, as my counselor pointed out. She's pretty nice. I had the feeling she thought Mr. Grisham was a jerk too but couldn't say it. She asked me about college and I told her I was thinking it over. "Definitely do," she said. I couldn't talk about my parents, at least not yet. I don't know why. I never talk about my parents, except to Kelly and now to you.

It's interesting what you said about depression and the mind shutting down to give itself a rest. My mind could probably use a rest. It's always rushing ahead, trying to solve problems even before they happen and trying to think every unthinkable thought. And that made me think about Isabel Archer and why she probably got married. I think she did it because her mind is a lot like mine. When a time came when she didn't know what to do with it next, she did the first useful thing that came along. Or what seemed like a useful thing. She thought she was helping Pansy and she thought she was helping Osmond, so she just did it, because helping is better than drifting.

This is very scary, because I could see me doing something just as stupid. I'm going to work hard not to, ever. I have two dreams: to be a writer and to have a place of my own that's beautiful and still (I love the word "still"). If I ever did get married (and I can't imagine *that*), it would be to someone who wanted me to have those things too. It was the scariest thing ever to read James's description of how Osmond wanted Isabel's mind "to be his—attached to his own like a small garden-plot to a deer-park. He would rake the soil gently and water the flowers; he would weed the beds and gather an occasional nosegay. It would be a pretty piece of property for a proprietor already far-reaching. He didn't wish her to be stupid. On the contrary, it was because she was clever that she had pleased him. But he expected her intelligence to operate altogether in his favour, and so far from desiring her mind to be a blank he had flattered himself that it would be richly receptive."

Now that I've gotten over the shock of Isabel's marriage, I'm back to loving James. Isn't that a perfect, horrible vision: her mind like a small garden-plot? And now I think James did shoot her down so suddenly for a reason. Because it's supposed to shock us and make us think. At least that's my interpretation.

Well, anyway, thank you again a million times for calling me yesterday. I feel so much better about so many things. No more Mr. Grisham! I'll try to get back to writing soon and send you a new chapter.

Love,
Liz

Dear Journal of One Who's Survived—
    —because I've dropped Mr. Grisham (I picture him hanging out of a fourth-floor window before I let him go!). It's all because of Julia, who actually called me on the phone (!!!) and encouraged me to talk to my guidance counselor. Which I did. The counselor was really nice and is the one who helped me drop *(smash, crack, crunch)* the monster. Thank you, God and Guidance. And Journal and Julia.

October 10, 1995

Dear Liz,

It was lovely talking to you, too. It is fun wondering what someone looks like when you know only her mind. I have a very definite picture of you, and also based on nothing. Maybe one of these days we'll meet.

It's nice to have a letter that sounds like Liz again. If you ever get truly depressed for a long time, you should take it seriously and ask for help. But short depressions are useful sometimes, I think, at least for me. My mind seems to ask me to stop now and then and sort things out, and I'm usually stronger for it if I do just that. The problem with the business world is you can't ever really stop, you just run on automatic. After a while nothing seems meaningful when you can do it in your sleep, so to speak.

What lovely dreams you have. I hope you'll follow them, always. Some people manage it. My mother was a fairly successful painter, and my father taught first grade in a day when men never did. (Do they now?)

He was offered lots of other jobs both in teaching and administration, but he was never swayed. He loved little kids. One of the things I'm more and more aware of, sorting through my parents' things, is how happy these two were. Their lives were all of a piece. Not all grown-ups are miserable, Liz, and I think the ones who aren't are the ones following dreams. You're right about James making a point. Isabel didn't have to marry Osmond, did she? Maybe she just gave up on her dreams too soon. It seems as if most people do.

Who will your new English teacher be? I imagine Mr. Grisham will be disappointed when he finds out you've dropped his class. My guess is he actually believed he was providing some sort of necessary service by tormenting you. The only time my father was ever tempted to go into administration was when it occurred to him *he* could torment such teachers and possibly force them out of teaching.

I've just reread your last chapter. It was far better than you think. I can see how it grew out of your anger and depression, and that's not a bad thing. In fact, writing is a good thing to do with that anger and depression if you do it honestly and have a gift, as you surely do. I could use an outlet lately for mine. I'm afraid I'm taking it out on a few of my authors who are trying graciously not to complain but must be having bad dreams.

Please call me if you ever need to talk, Liz. My phone number here is (703) 555–2649.

Love to you,
Julia

Dear Journal of Someone With a Gift and
Without Mr. Grisham,

I have a new English teacher and she's
actually even good. Compared to Mr.
Grisham, she's just perfect. If I'm ever a
teacher, I hope I know how to criticize people in a way that helps them GROW,
instead of just hurting them. How can they
let Mr. Grisham teach?

I believe a teacher should be like Julia,
who knows how to say things in a way
that makes you work and think. A way that
makes you believe in your gift and want to
improve it. She thinks she's being hard on
her authors, but I'm sure she isn't. I'll bet
that whatever she's saying is just what they
need to hear, like it or not.

Julia is perfect. And *I* have her phone
number! A privilege I'll never abuse.

October 15, 1995

Dear Julia,

I was amazed you liked my last chapter,
but when I went back and read it and
thought about what you said about my anger
and depression being in there, I *saw* it. It
was really weird. If you'd told me to sit
down and put my anger into a book, I
wouldn't have known how to do it. Now I
like the chapter too.

I loved hearing about your parents and
their beautiful life together. They're just the
kind of parents I used to dream of having.
Your childhood must have been perfect. No
wonder you can't throw things out. How is
your father doing? I feel so sorry for you.

My new English teacher is Mrs. Breiner.
She's really nice. Her class is pretty boring,
but it's not her fault. The kids aren't interested and their skills are weak (to put it
kindly), so she spends a lot of time going
over the same stuff. The nice thing about it
is she appreciates me because I *am* interested.
We talk a lot after class. She's letting me

write my paper on *The Portrait of a Lady*,
even though I've already read the book. Mr.
Grisham would have called that cheating.
Mrs. Breiner knows I'm not trying to get out
of work but trying to learn more about what
really interests me.

The only bad thing is that Kelly's in the
class, and I can tell that I annoy her. She
thinks I'm showing off. I've stopped worrying about what Kelly thinks. I'm not showing off.

I hope you're fine. Thanks for sending
your phone number. I will call you one day
but only for something special. I don't want
to abuse the privilege!

Love,
Liz

Dear Journal,

I've spent all of today working on a chapter where I have Elspeth and her mother flip out and do something completely outrageous, something my real-life mother would do without a blink but that I'd never go along with in one million years. But Elspeth does go along, and while I'm having her do it, part of me is thinking how much fun it would be to act like this and just go with my emotions. While I was writing, I actually comprehended my mother. She just loves throwing things, I can tell she does, and until I wrote this chapter, I never understood why. Not that I approve, of course, but I can at least grasp the impulse, especially when a person has no other talents or way to express things. (Did I just call throwing things a talent??)

Dear Journal,

Julia's into silence again. I have my chapter finished, and guess I'll just go on and send it.

Kelly came over today and we went to a movie. She drives now, which is more than a little depressing. It's like there's one more way she's part of the world of people and doing stuff while I'm only part of the world of thinking (and sometimes writing). No wonder we bore each other. Though I wasn't really bored today. We laughed a lot at the movie and also at her driving—Journal, she is really bad!

November 12, 1995

Dear Julia,

I'm kind of worried because you haven't answered my letter, but you're probably really busy. Maybe you had to fly to New York? I read about a Matisse exhibit there. I hope you got to see it. I thought about asking my father if we could go, but he's been in such a bad mood lately, I decided not to bother. Anyway, he hates New York City. He says it's where King Kong went to die. (Whatever *that* means.)

I dread Thanksgiving. Holidays here are bizarre. My mom's sister, Louise, comes to visit with her husband Ron (Ron's part-time job is to be a singing banana—need I say more?). My Grandpa Beech comes over from Pittsburgh. He's nice but never really talks, just like you-know-who. He and Dad will watch football while my mother bangs things around the kitchen and swears. It's all pretty weird. Mom uses both of the kitchens to cook in, so we'll have turkey at Dad's and go to Mom's for dessert.

I wonder where you'll be for Thanksgiving. Probably with your father. When I think about that, it makes me feel childish for complaining.

Here's one more chapter. It will probably be the last for a while. We have exams before Christmas, and I have to study a lot. Also, my brother might be coming home, which may be a problem or may be nice, but either way it will use up some energy.

Happy Thanksgiving. (Or as happy as possible.) Write soon.

Love,
Liz

Chapter Six

"LET'S GO SHOPPING," Elspeth's mother said one day with a happy, mischievous look on her face. It was a look Elspeth hadn't seen in a long time. Lately her mother had regressed from angry back to sad.

"Shopping for what?" Elspeth felt a twinge of foreboding. "And with what?" Her mother was broke. They both knew that.

"For a present for Patsy." Her mother smiled. "And with your father's money. I think she'd like something very big and very ugly. Don't you? And very, very, expensive."

Elspeth's mouth fell open.

"Right?" her mother went on. "Don't you think she deserves a gift like that? A truly special gift."

Elspeth closed her mouth. She tried to look disapproving. "What do you mean? How would we get Dad's money?" But even as she asked it, she knew the answer. He kept a credit card hidden in his dresser drawer. It would be simple. "And what's the point? To make Patsy think Dad has bad taste? Or wants to insult her or something?"

Her mother shrugged. "Maybe. Or to make him think she used his card to buy herself something big. Either way."

"But they'll tell each other. They'll each say they didn't buy it."

Her mother smiled. "So what? Who can they accuse? I can't get into the house, and *you* wouldn't do such a thing!"

Elspeth smiled too in spite of herself. True. Good old upright Elspeth, mother of all adults, would never do such a thing.

"Okay. Let's go shopping," she said.

The next morning they watched for her dad and Patsy to go off to work. While her mother called the school to say Elspeth was sick, Elspeth stole the card. She felt guilty, reaching into her father's drawer and lifting up his T-shirts. But then she saw the nightgown, nestled down into the drawer. Patsy's nightgown. So much for guilt. She grabbed the card and ran.

It took a whole morning of shopping to find exactly the right thing, but they knew it when they saw it, gleaming across the import store.

"What is it?" Elspeth asked.

Her mother laughed. They stared at the thing in wonder. It was almost as tall as they were and silver in color. Bright, shiny, silver.

"A tree?" her mother guessed. It was as good a guess as any. Silver birds dotted the thing here and there. And what appeared to be a silver squirrel hung from one of the silver branches.

"A tree would be a very good gift," Elspeth offered. "Patsy's a nature lover—except for cats."

"Yes," her mother agreed. "And the price is certainly right." She held up the tag: $420.00.

When it came time to sign the charge slip, they looked at each other. Elspeth's mother took the pen. "Patsy Bishop Nicholson," she wrote in round, upright letters. Just like Patsy's.

It took both of them to get it up her father's stairs, but at the doorway Elspeth stopped her mother. A joke was one thing. Letting her mother into her father's house was another.

Her mother frowned but agreed to wait outside while Elspeth worked the statue across the floor to the center of the room. Carefully, she replaced the credit card exactly where she'd found it.

"I do hope they'll like it," her mother said, once they were safely home.

Elspeth started to laugh. They both laughed so hard that tears ran down their cheeks. Laughing until they cried.

Dear Journal,

Today was Thanksgiving and worse than anything you'll have imagined. Worse even than my birthday, if you can believe that. Roger didn't come home and didn't tell us he wasn't coming until this morning. Aunt Louise and Uncle Ron did come, of course, and Ron brought a cake that was shaped like a turkey on a platter—but a turkey whose body was also a football. It had ice cream cones for the legs. All very clever. Of course what happened was everyone loved it and ate it and ignored my mother's pies. Not good, since she was already mad at Ron for saying that eating her creamed onions was like eating giant eyeballs, which made everyone laugh but also gag and stop eating the onions. So after staring awhile at her pies, my mother attacked what was left of the cake with a huge carving knife (asking "Who wants the white meat?") and splattered the whole thing. My mother is NUTS. But such good material. Tonight I started a really funny chapter, the only good part of the day.

Journal, I haven't heard from Julia. I think something must be wrong. Should I call her and wish her Happy Thanksgiving? Part of me wants to, but part of me feels afraid. Afraid of what?

November 26, 1995

Dear Liz,

I can't imagine what you think, my waiting so long to answer your letter and to comment on Chapter Six. I'm sorry, but I know you'll understand when I tell you that my father died on October 18.

It was a great shock to me, despite his failing health. Only the day before he'd laughed aloud at something I'd said, and that had seemed such a good sign. Of course the truth is there was no hope of recovery, and only worse illness lay ahead. Still, it was sad. Many people loved him and came to his funeral. They confirmed what I'd always thought—that my father was someone special.

But now I have no excuse: I must get to work on the house. In early November I went back to New York for a week to deal with pressing issues there. What a mess I left things in. And there's a mess here of paperwork and bills and still the house to clean and sell. I'm trying to be ruthless. If I sort and discard things now, I can put the house up for sale in the spring. It's all very depressing, but in the course of making decisions, a cheerful thought occurred to me—would you consider coming to visit over your Christmas vacation? I'm going to put up a tree and have myself one last Christmas at home. It would be a lovely way for us to meet and celebrate our friendship if you could come share this time with me. What do you think? I'd be happy to talk to your father and happy to pay the cost. Shockingly, my father was well insured and I am fairly well off.

Your chapter is terrific, very fresh and funny. I can't wait to see where you're headed. If you come, we can discuss it. I'm curious to know if you've worked out a plan for your book or whether you're a fly-by-the-seat-of-your-pants kind of writer.

Let me know as soon as possible what your thoughts are. Christmas flights are difficult to book. You may have to take the train, a bit more time-consuming but a very pretty ride. It should be easy for you to travel from Philadelphia to either Clifton Forge or Lynchburg.

I look forward to hearing from you. If the trip is impossible, I'll understand.

Love,
Julia

Dear Julia,

Oh my gosh! I'm so, so sorry. I wish I
had known that your father died. Not that
you needed *me*, but it makes me sad to think
that I might have at least called you and told
you how much I cared, the way you called
me when it mattered.

It's so unbelievable that you want me to
come to your parents' wonderful house, but
Julia, MY FATHER WON'T LET ME DO
IT. I hate him. I hate him so much it hurts.
I told him if I don't go you'll have to have
your last Christmas in your parents' house
alone, and he said that that's really not his
problem. He's such a jerk. I asked him why,
when you're paying my way, he thinks he
can just say "no," and he says he can say it
because he's my father. Rational, right? He
says he doesn't even know you. I said that *I*
know you and that he could talk to you on
the phone, but it didn't make any difference.

I tried talking to my mother, but that
was no use. She's in a bad mood because of

Thanksgiving. (Nobody helped her cook, then my uncle made fun of the onions and my brother didn't come, etc. etc. etc. All so important, right?) Not that I blame her. My mother's life stinks. But she never stops thinking about it long enough to give any thought to me. She says yes, my father's acting like a jerk, but then he always acts like a jerk, so it's what I should expect, and that she's not about to talk to him when she doesn't really have to. An injustice to me isn't any kind of reason, of course.

Julia, I'm not giving up. I'm going to pester my father until he has to give me a reason. A real, true reason. And he doesn't have one.

Thank you so much, Julia. I can't believe you really asked me. If you can send me advice, I'll take it.

Love,
Liz

November 30, 1995

Dear Julia,

Help! I need that advice quickly. My
father says if I don't stop talking about going
to Virginia, he's going to lock me up in my
bedroom and only let me out for school,
which I wouldn't actually mind except that I
couldn't bug him to change his mind. Julia, I
can't just give up. What do you think I
should do?

Love,
Liz

December 4, 1995

Dear Liz,

I'm alarmed to hear I've caused so much drama in Edgewood Heights. I've decided to write your father. A phone call seemed too aggressive. (Or maybe I'm just a coward!) I sent off a letter today explaining who I am and why I know you and how much I hope you can come. I don't know if it will do any good, but I'll keep my fingers crossed.

If, after that, he says no, Liz, I think you should let it drop. Rational or not, he is your father. We can still meet one day.

Love,
Julia

December 7, 1995

Dear Julia,

I think your letter to my father arrived in the same mail with mine. My father hasn't said anything yet, but he keeps looking at me weirdly. I think that maybe there's hope. A tiny ray of hope.

Here's the new chapter. I wish I could be as quick and witty as Elspeth. I don't understand how her great lines can just pop out of my head and onto paper when they'd never pop out of me. In real life I'm pretty shy, even with my parents. If I could be Elspeth for just one day, I would definitely get to Virginia!

Love,
Liz

Chapter Seven

"ELSPETH?" IT WAS HER FATHER, on the phone. "You wouldn't happen to know anything about this monstrosity in my living room, would you?"

"You mean Patsy?" Elspeth smiled into the phone.

"Look, young lady. This isn't funny. Not if somebody paid what I think they paid for this piece of junk."

"Why would you think it was me? I don't have any money."

"I hate to say this, Elspeth, but I want you to return the key you have to my house. It's a sad day when a father can't trust a daughter."

"And when a mother can't trust her friend?"

"Bring me the key."

"I think I'll mail it." Elspeth hung up the phone.

"They didn't like their present," she told her mother.

Her mother was lying on her bed, staring up at the ceiling. Elspeth worried when she did that. It usually meant she was plotting.

"Oh, really?" Her mother sat up. "Maybe we should get them another."

"Can't. Dad wants his key back. Anyway, by now he'll have hidden his credit card. He might be an idiot, but he's not stupid."

"Yes." Her mother looked thoughtful. "He's an idiot but he's not stupid. But you know we don't actually need the credit card as long as we have the number."

"Do we have the number?"

Her mother rolled her eyes. "Elspeth, of course we do." She pointed at her temple. "And this time shopping will be so simple. No lugging things around or making any deliveries."

"Mom, what are you talking about?"

Her mother bolted off the bed and into the TV room. "Home shopping, of course."

They started out with some basics—an onion chopper for Patsy and an electric garage door opener for her father. "You never know when he might decide to build a garage," pointed out Elspeth's mother.

But basics were boring. They bought Patsy a trip for one to Rio de Janeiro, where she would be less bored.

"Oh, look!" said Elspeth's mother. "And there's the bathing suit she should wear!" It was an ugly mustard color with an old-lady-like skirt. They hurried to buy her that.

For Elspeth's father a stuffed canary, to go with the silver tree. "This bird theme is nice," said Elspeth. Her mother agreed. They bought an antique birdcage, then fifty pounds of seed.

For Patsy a bust exerciser so she'd look nice in her bathing suit.

"And how about something for ourselves?" her mother suggested. A diamond necklace was twinkling on the screen.

"Mom—" Elspeth suddenly started to worry. "Isn't this all illegal?"

"Of course it is, honey."

"Well then let's stop."

"Why?" Her mother looked genuinely surprised. "You think your father will have you arrested? You, his only child?"

"He might have *you* arrested."

"Not likely. I'm the mother of that child. You'd beg him not to. I could plead insanity, too."

Elspeth sighed. "I guess that would hold up in court."

"Right. Now let's get on with things." She was hurrying to the phone. "Your father would buy Patsy that necklace in a minute if she asked him to."

It was true. Elspeth remembered how he'd been washing the dishes and how he'd waxed Patsy's car last weekend, when he'd never once waxed her mother's. He and Patsy went out for dinner all the time.

"Look, Mom!" She pointed to the screen. "There's a bracelet to go with it!"

Her mother smiled. When she hung up the phone, she sighed in contentment. "That'll have to be it for today. We've maxed out our credit line."

"Impressive achievement, I'd say!"

Her mother nodded and shrugged non-chalantly. "All in a day's work," she said.

December 8, 1995

Dear Julia,

   A miracle happened today. My father
and I had a talk. The real kind of talk where
the other person listens. He told me he'd
had a letter from you and that you sounded
very nice. He asked about my writing and I
told him the bare essentials—how it was
important to me and how you made me feel
very special. It was weird. He started to look
really sad and then he said he was glad for
me. (!!)
   Anyway, he's thinking it over. Julia, I
think from my father that's a yes! I know it's
getting late to make the arrangements, but
the minute I know, I'll call.

                    Love,
                    Liz

December 9, 1995

Dear Julia,

I can't believe this is happening! I'm sorry I talked so long last night. It just all seems so unreal, that I'm going to meet you at last and that I'm going to see your parents' house and that I'm going to get to travel.

The only bad part is my father's driving me. I know I should be grateful and that it will get me there faster, but it definitely spoils some of the fun. I'd rather take the train. It is nice of him, though, and I think he's excited too, even though he won't admit it. He doesn't travel any more than I do (of course it's his own fault). He's planning to go on to Richmond and visit his "Army buddy," so he won't be in our way.

According to Dad, traffic will be awful on the weekend before Christmas, so we're going to leave on the 22nd and come home on the 28th. I pointed out that you'd invited me for a whole week, but Dad says he can't manage to take that much time off and that he'll already have to work twenty-four hours a day to get ready to go. I didn't think I should mention that his presence wasn't required in the first place. Mom isn't thrilled about my being away for Christmas, but she has a sort-of-boyfriend at the moment, so she'll be okay. She hardly even asked any questions about you. Once she heard you were an editor and I was writing a book, she got this look on her face like I'd just started singing opera or talking about war—sort of a surprised and alarmed and bored look all at the same time.

Dad and I have maps out all over the place. You'd think we were charting a polar expedition. If I weren't going somewhere I'm so anxious to get to, I'd like to travel without maps—just drive and see what happens. I guess that's why I'm a fly-by-the-seat-of-my-pants kind of writer!

See you soon!!

Love,
Liz

Dear Journal,

Everything I ever hoped would happen in my life is happening. An interesting, *professional* person has read my writing and shared her thoughts with me and *invited me to visit*.

Yes, dear Journal, next week I leave for Virginia. The only bad thing is that my father leaves for Virginia with me. But I'm going to block him out. As far as I'm concerned, he's only my dull-witted driver. I'm sorry that I've ignored you—there's just so much going on: exams, Christmas shopping, and PLANNING A TRIP TO VIRGINIA. But I promise to take you with me. You're now the Journal of a Writer Who Gets to Travel.

December 13, 1995

Dear Liz,

This is exciting for me too, believe me.
I'm actually very grateful to your father for
driving you down, even if it spoils some of
your fun. Now I won't have to worry about
your traveling alone on the train. I know
you'd do fine, but still, I'd worry. Also, I
think it will be good for him to meet me and
put any final worries to rest. You'll have
plenty of opportunities in your lifetime to
travel. This is a small but good beginning.
Maybe while you're here we can take a day
trip or two if the weather's right.

I can't decide whether to decorate my
house before you come so that it will be
Christmasy when you get here or whether to
save the fun for us to share. Maybe I'll do
half and half.

Have a safe trip. I'll be home all day on
the 22nd, so whenever you arrive is fine. If
the weather forecast is threatening, please
adjust your plans. Tell your father he's welcome to stay for dinner before going on. (Or

don't tell him, as you see fit!) You should be flattered by his concern, Liz. He must really care.

Love,
Julia

P.S. By the way, I loved your chapter. It is very witty and funny. One day you will be too when you outgrow being shy.

Dear Journal of a Happy Person Who Will
One Day Be Witty and Funny,

I think I flunked a math exam, but do I
care? No, I don't. And Kelly said, "Let's not
exchange presents this year." But do I care?
No, I don't. Only one thing matters at this
particular moment, and we both know what
that is.

12/27/95

Dear Journal of a Person Who Now Knows
Bliss,

Did you know you're in Virginia? I
brought you here so I could record every
single thought of what it's like to travel, but
I've been so busy I haven't had time to
write. I think that even if I had had the time,
I couldn't have found the words. Henry
James would have found them all right, but
Liz from New Jersey can't. This whole week
is like some kind of magic, a big beautiful

bubble that I'm scared might pop. Julia is everything I wanted her to be and so is Virginia.

Today we drove to Charlottesville and visited Monticello and the University of Virginia. It's the most beautiful school, with buildings designed by Thomas Jefferson. Julia says there's an excellent English department, but it's very hard to get into, especially if you live out of state. I might try, though. For the first time college really does seem important.

The only bad thing that's happened was that on Christmas Eve day we went to the cemetery so Julia could leave wreaths on her parents' graves. She started crying and I felt like I shouldn't be there. I didn't know what to say. It was pretty upsetting, but as soon as we left, Julia returned to normal and even told some jokes. We went back to her house and had eggnog and strung popcorn for the tree. It was the kind of thing that would have felt corny if I did it in New Jersey. (No pun intended!)

And Christmas morning was just unreal. Julia had wrapped up lots of little presents for me and put them under the tree: a fountain pen; a copy of a beautiful book of children's poems edited by Julia (her favorite project at Springtime); postcards of paintings by Matisse; some lovely-smelling hand cream. But the most amazing present of all was a framed painting that was done years ago by her mother. Journal, it's the most beautiful thing—so beautiful it made me cry. Can you believe Julia wants me to have something made by her mother? This is all like a dream.

I felt bad because I only had two presents for her: a box of candy (sounds ordinary, I know, but there was a Matisse painting on the box), and a set of antique bookends that were made out of bronze with a child reading a book carved into them. They cost a LOT of money, but Dad agreed I should buy them since Julia was having me stay at her house and they were partly a hostess gift. He even gave me $20 towards them. (!?!)

Dad has been so weird. He was really nice at dinner with Julia, and even the ride down wasn't all that bad. He seemed to change when we got away from New Jersey—to sort of relax. He never does relax, now that I think about it. Maybe that's one of his problems.

Well, dear Journal, it's time to go to bed. I can't believe that tomorrow I'll have to go back to New Jersey. I wish I could stay in this place forever. It's so strange—*here* seems like where I'm supposed to be and home seems like a dream (a very *bad* dream). That other person, the one who's forced to live there, is really not me but someone who is dreaming. I wish I'd wake up and be set free.

Dear Julia,

How could I ever thank you, even in a million years? It seems impossible that it's all already over and we're back here in New Jersey.

Everything was too perfect for words. I love your parents' house, even more than Shana's apartment—a hundred times more—and I can tell I would have loved your parents. It's so weird that you look like I imagined—pretty, with long dark hair tied back. You look professional and elegant, but soft and friendly too. I wish I could look that way instead of being so sloppy and bony.

I loved all of my gifts, also, especially the little painting you gave me that your mother did. I'll treasure it forever. I went right to the library and took out a book on the Dutch school of art. I think you're right that her paintings are like those—perfectly still and lovely. I hold my breath when I look at them, as if I could accidentally blow their beauty away. I especially love the Vermeers.

Your mother's paintings are a lot like his, but her women are so definitely modern. I love the way the rooms are *there*, in perfect detail, looking as if time could never change them. Like perfect, beautiful little time capsules.

My father drove me crazy all the way home, asking questions about the week. I appreciated his interest, but I didn't want to tell him a thing. I wanted to hold everything about you and your house perfectly still at my center, as if your mother had painted it there. It's hard to explain, since for years I've hated my father for not asking about things that matter to me! I kept switching the conversation to his week with his Army buddy, and he actually talked a lot. MY FATHER WAS IN A GOOD MOOD! He told me all these crazy things he and his friend did when they were young and in the Army. You know, my father once had a life—who ever would have guessed?

Anyway, thank you again for everything. I don't know how I can ever repay you for the best week in my life. Thanks, too, for all your suggestions about Elspeth. I have so many ideas. I can't wait to get to work, but

school has started, so it may be a while
before I have something to send you. My
New Year's resolution is to finish the book.

Thank you, thank you, thank you, and
love (and happy New Year!)—

Liz

P.S. My father says thanks for both of those
dinners and to say you're a great Southern
cook. I agree! And he's sorry he showed up
so late on Thursday that we had to stay the
night. I hated having him there, but it was
worth it to get to have an extra day with
you. Anything would have been.

Dear Liz,

Happy New Year to you, too.

You owe me no thanks. If you could only
know how much it meant to me to share my
last Christmas in my parents' house with
someone who appreciated it so genuinely.
And I loved giving you my mother's painting. One of the sad things about not having
children is thinking that families come to the
end of the line. When I die, who will there
be to remember or care, or to value the
things that once meant something to us? But
of course my parents' lives were their own
and complete in themselves. What do their
things matter now that they're gone? Still, I
loved giving that one thing to you.

How perceptive of you to pick out
Vermeer. Yes, I've always thought myself
that my mother's work echoed his. I don't
know whether my mother knew his work or
not. She never took much of an academic
interest in art. Never even studied, really.
She just stayed in her house and worked,

which is probably what Vermeer did himself. All of the trappings in his paintings, the maps and such, are objects that he owned.

I must confess to thinking your father very nice. He was on his best behavior, of course, but he strikes me as being genuinely concerned about you. He also seems rather lonely. But I don't presume to know on such slim observation what's really the truth about him. Father-daughter relations are tricky and personal, and who am I to judge? I only know that he does seem to love you.

I'll be here until the end of the month, so send whatever you write. I hope 1996 is a fruitful, exciting, happy year for you. Thanks again for the chocolates and the extraordinary and beautiful bookends. I'm taking them back to New York, where they'll decorate my desk at work (presuming some surface remains).

Love,
Julia

P.S. You're far from sloppy and bony. You're a beautiful, blossoming young woman, as I had pictured you! These days, I fear, it's I who am sloppy and bony. My hair is pulled back because I don't bother to style it and I've lost fourteen pounds in the last two months by simply worrying it away.

January 9, 1996

Dear Julia,

I had no idea you'd lost fourteen pounds! That doesn't sound healthy. Please take care of yourself.

Thank you for the compliments. It's funny, you make me *feel* as if one day I might become a beautiful woman. You make me feel as if anything is possible and that I might really do something in the world that matters. No one, not even Mrs. Reeves, could make me feel it, even though she always said it.

Maybe my father does love me in his weird way, but he's never been very convincing. It seems to me that parents should do for their children what yours did for you (what *you* do for me) and make them feel strong and sure of themselves. My parents only make me feel crazy and angry and confused. And I can't tell my father anything important, because he never tells me what he thinks. He just looks like he wishes I'd stop talking. Or else he overreacts and makes mountains out of molehills so I'm sorry I brought things up. Everything is nothing or a very big deal. Anyway, it hardly seems to matter now. Soon I'll be out in the world, like you are.

I'm working on a chapter, but it's not done yet. I'm not sure exactly what should happen to Elspeth and her mother. My own mother seemed really lonesome when we got home. I think her new boyfriend dumped her. She's so emotional. I feel older than her sometimes—like it wasn't right of us to leave her alone in the house for so long. Or am I confusing her with Elspeth's mother???

Please write soon. I miss you. My father thinks it's dumb that we write letters back and forth. He says, "Pick up the phone and call. We can afford it." It made me think about how important the letters *are*. I hope we never stop writing.

Love,
Liz

January 12, 1996

Dear Liz,

Your father doesn't understand that he's
the father of a literary figure yet, that's all.
No one today writes letters.

I'm happy to think that I've been a help
to you. You've been a help to me, too. Not
only do you make me remember how it felt
to be young, but, curiously, you make me
remember my parents more clearly. I lately
remember that we fought very, very often
when I was your age. I was a know-it-all
teenager, not shy at all. I wonder how my
father maintained his unflagging patience
and sense of humor. I suppose, being a
teacher, he was used to it all.

Since I've never had children, I'm no
authority on the parent-child relationship,
but I do know that it's much harder for a
parent to give a child the kind of advice an
outsider can give and have it listened to.
Things are a big deal to your father because
he doesn't have the luxury of distance and
objectivity. I hope the two of you can make

peace one of these days. And I hope you'll learn to know your mother, whoever she is. The parent thing doesn't end when you're grown, believe me. Here I am sorting through drawers, remembering, feeling remorse over this and joy over that as if it all happened yesterday. We carry our parents with us forever, I think.

Anyway, enough about that. I have some rather extraordinary news. In all the confusion of things it seems I forgot a commitment I'd made over a year ago in—of all places!— Philadelphia! I'm signed up to be a visiting lecturer at Temple University for a week, beginning January 29th. Thank goodness I finally opened the pile of mail forwarded from the office. It's a wonder they still bother.

I know you're close to Philadelphia, and I'm hoping we can manage another visit or two. I'd be happy to come to you if you can tell me how to do so, or you can come to me. I'll be arriving on the 26th and staying at the Latham Hotel at 17th and Walnut. On Saturday I have to attend a meeting, but Sunday the 28th is free. How about for you?

So much for progress here. Now I'm

frantic trying to put together a program, the sort of thing I could do in my sleep in my New York City life. Was it only months ago?

Let me know if we can work something out.

Love,
Julia

Dear Journal of a Literary Figure,

Julia is going to come here, TO MY
HOUSE. Part of me's embarrassed, but the
other part is thrilled. I know Julia won't
judge me by where I live. It's so weird that
her trip to Philadelphia was planned more
than a year ago. It's just fate.

January 16, 1996

Dear Julia,

The 28th is great! Wow! This is a wonderful surprise.

Either way transportation isn't a problem because my father says he'll drive us in and out of the city. He thinks it would be rude of us not to have you to the house for dinner after all you did for me. I know he's right and I love the idea of showing you my room and where I hung your mother's picture, but it means including my father in everything. There's no way that won't spoil your visit (a lot!) even if we all get along. And no doubt Mom will make an entrance you'll never forget.

Dad is already planning the dinner he wants to cook (he only does this for women *other* than family members), so I guess I can't say no. Maybe after dinner we can "retire" to my room and he'll butt out. Or maybe you have a reason I should come to you? Hint, hint.

Let me know what you think. I'm so

excited that you're coming. The thought of having you in my house, even with my father, is thrilling. I can't *picture* you here.

Love,
Liz

January 20, 1996

Dear Liz,

What I think is that if your father doesn't mind all the driving, you should come into the city early and spend the day with me. I recall wonderful art museums in Philly. Then we'll go out to your house and have dinner with your father. That should make everyone happy.

I'll call you when I get to Philadelphia. You and your father plan whatever works best for you and causes the least inconvenience. The day is yours.

Love,
Julia

Dear Journal of the Daughter of an Asshole,

I can't believe it—my father put the moves on Julia when she was here. Oh, he was subtle. Almost clever. I don't think she even suspected. But whatever he did, it worked, because Julia thinks he's nice. Can you believe it? It's just spoiled everything. Before we came back to the house for dinner, we'd been having this perfectly wonderful time. Now I can't even think about that. I can only think of how Julia raved about this man's stupid linguine and drank his dumb red wine and how my father told two actually funny stories which I had never even heard.

I'll never forgive him, he's lower than a worm. It will change everything if my father becomes friends with Julia. (It will never be more than friends, of course. Julia is not *dumb*.)

February 6, 1996

Dear Liz,

Now it's time for me to thank you for a
very special time. I loved every minute of
our time together: the beautiful little museum designed by Frank Furness, our long
lunch together, and of course the evening at
your house. I'm going to write to your father
separately to thank him for the dinner. I
found it rather touching, I must confess, that
he would go to so much trouble.

I've been thinking a lot about our discussions of your father and trying to put what I
hear together with what I see. I hope you
won't mind my saying that I think the two
of you misread each other a lot. Your father
seems rather shy to me. I think perhaps he
senses and respects your talents and feels
intimidated. At the very least, he's interested
in your future. I can tell by the questions
that he asked me.

I must say I can't put him together with
your mother, although my visit with her was
brief and I probably shouldn't judge. She

seemed emotional, as you said, and a little overwhelming. Your father has two strong women in his life—you in a positive way and your mother in a negative one—and I suspect he's weak in the asserting-himself department. That's how I read it, for whatever it's worth.

It was nice of both of you to drive me to the airport on Saturday. The flight home was uneventful, and it *was* a coming "home." After all these years I don't think of New York as my home. How curious. It also occurs to me that when I get back to New York, I won't be so far away from you—a two-hour train ride at most. A nice thought.

Write when you can. Thank you again for everything. Regards to your father.

Love,
Julia

Dear Journal,

Did you know that my father is *frightened* by me and my mother? Oh yes, it seems that he's "rather shy." Well the poor old thing.

I suppose he should be frightened. I'd like to punch his nose in.

February 12, 1996

Dear Liz,

Why haven't I heard from you since I've
been home? Are you upset with me in some
way? I did notice that you were silent in the
car on the way to the airport, but I attributed
it to the fact that your father was there and
he and I were in the front with our backs to
you. Now I'm worrying that it might be more
than that. Liz, please let me know. I feel
strangely unsure of myself lately. I was such a
flop at Temple. I wasn't relevant to their class
and couldn't seem to adjust. It was very dis-
concerting. Anyway, I hope I haven't upset
you by saying or doing something stupid and
being too dense to know it.

My job seems to be at risk so, ready or
not, I have to go back to New York. I don't
feel ready. My experience at Temple makes
me think I can no longer fly by the seat of
my pants when the pressure's on. In short,
I'm afraid, and fear is not a useful emotion
for navigating the New York waters.

Please do write when you have time.

I know you're busy, but just a note to let me know you're all right would make me very happy. I'll let you know when I change my address. I'm going to close up the house and let it sit empty awhile.

Love,
Julia

February 15, 1996

Dear Julia,

I'm sorry I haven't written. I guess I was
a little upset about something, but it was
stupid of me and now I want to forget it.
I'm sorry. Don't even wonder about it.

I had a wonderful time in Philadelphia
with you. I can't believe we live so close to
important art museums and never, ever, go.
I complained about this to my dad and he
said, "Well, let's do it!" I'll believe that when
I see it—*Dad* in an art museum?!

You have a very weird picture of my
father. He isn't shy or intimidated. He just
doesn't really care—not enough to say what
he thinks or to be involved. He wants to go
around with his head in some business
cloud. Since our vacation he's been his same
old self. Don't even think about him.

I'm sorry you have to go back to New
York when you don't want to. It doesn't
seem fair that you can't take time off to be
sad when both of your parents die, especially
when they were wonderful parents, like

yours were. I don't know why you're scared, though. You're so clever and smart. I'll bet you were wonderful at Temple. You just don't know it.

I saw that your thank-you note came to my father. He didn't let me read it, but it was nice of you to write. You didn't have to do it, though.

I've almost finished a chapter. Tell me where to send it.

Love,
Liz

February 19, 1996

Dear Liz,

Send it to the office in New York and mark it "personal." Like it or not, I'm on my way back. I'll be in touch as soon as I've settled in. Also, please thank your father for *his* nice letter. It was charming and funny. You must get some of your talent from him. I hope to see both of you one of these days soon.

Love,
Julia

Dear Journal,

I guess I really am crazy. I thought
Julia's letter said that I GET MY TALENT
FROM MY FATHER. I must be mistaken,
but I'll never know for sure since I ripped it
up as soon as I got it.

One good thing happened, though. All of
my anger at that letter helped me finish
Chapter Eight, which is about betrayal. Not
that I can really think of Julia as a betrayer.
She thinks she's helping me by saying nice
things about my father. She doesn't understand that my getting together with my
father isn't important to me—my getting
away from him is. She's supposed to be on
the *away* side of the fence.

Dear Julia,

If my father wrote you a note that was charming and funny, it must have been plagiarized. My father can't even spell. You have such a weird picture of him. It's a little irritating, as if you don't believe a word I say to you. I don't think my father and I misread each other at all. I think you misread my father.

Here's Chapter Eight.

Liz

Chapter Eight

ELSPETH WAS TIRED of taking sides in the war between her parents. She agreed that her mother was crazy. She'd always been crazy, just like her father said.

At least that's what she thought on some days. On others she watched her father go in and out with Patsy and thought he had driven her mother crazy and then tried to blame her for it.

It was exhausting, choosing sides. They were both her parents; they were both often wrong. But lately her father was the most wrong. As she thought this, the truth suddenly hit Elspeth: the person to blame was Patsy. Before Patsy had gotten into the middle, she hadn't had to choose sides.

"I hate you," Elspeth whispered one afternoon. Patsy was out in her father's yard, reading a book in the sun. Elspeth watched her through the window. "I wish you would die." She didn't wish this, of course. Or maybe she did, but she'd never say it if wishes made things happen.

Didn't Patsy remember being best friends with Elspeth's mother when they were young? Didn't she remember sharing secrets and talking about things a person discussed only with special people? Once you did that, you shouldn't ever forget it. That person's enemy should be your enemy on principle alone.

It was time for Elspeth to say this, she decided. She slammed her window and rushed down the stairs to the yard.

Patsy didn't see her coming. "You're the lowest of the low," Elspeth whispered from right behind her chair.

Patsy jumped and dropped the book.

"You're lower than a worm."

Patsy sat up. Her face was red when she turned around. "I know you think that, Elspeth" was all she said.

"So?" Elspeth waited. She wanted to hear a good excuse. Patsy must at least think she had an excuse.

"So—nothing. This all just happened. And I feel bad about it. I feel *really* bad about it."

"Then stop seeing my father!" The answer

was pretty simple if Patsy felt all that bad.

Patsy sighed. "But I love your father, Elspeth."

"I thought you loved my mother."

Patsy's face turned even redder—a very unflattering color. "I did. I—do. But she didn't want your father. She doesn't want him now. Why should she care if I have him?"

"Why should she care if you have him?!" Elspeth couldn't believe she'd heard it. "I don't think this is somehow the point. The point is you can't have him and also have my mother, and *you chose him*."

Patsy looked embarrassed. After a minute she nodded. "Okay. I guess I did."

I hope you die, Elspeth thought again. She said, "So all those years of friendship didn't matter to you a bit? All those times you were siding with my mother when my parents got divorced—oh, you're just a hypocrite, Patsy!"

"Elspeth, that's not true. I *was* your mother's friend. I sympathized with her then and agreed with her lots of times too." Now Patsy looked angry.

"Until you fell in love?"

Patsy slammed her book shut. "I don't have to explain it to you, Elspeth."

"Yes, you do. Your clothes are in my closet. My pebbles are in your shoes."

Patsy looked surprised. "*You* did that?"

"Yes. And enjoyed it very much."

"Elspeth! I didn't think you were so vindictive. You'd better watch out. You'll grow up to be like your mother."

"Oh, so now you don't like my mother, who was only your lifelong friend. But you're not a hypocrite, right? Interesting theory."

Patsy stood up and clapped up the folding chair. "I can't talk to you," she said. "Not when you're acting like this." She stormed towards the house with the chair.

"Sure you can!" Elspeth called after her. "You can talk, but I'm not going to listen. Why would I listen to a betrayer? By the way—I hope you enjoy Rio!"

So now it was official: she was on her mother's side. There were lots of things Patsy might have said that would have made things a little better, but she hadn't chosen to say them. She hadn't said one. Not even that she was sorry.

Dear Liz,

I'm truly sorry if what I said about you and your father was insulting. I didn't intend it to be. Of course I believe everything you've told me about him. I only meant to point out that it's hard to be objective about situations when you're in them. I know I could have misread your father. I probably did. Lately I misread many things. But I *don't* think he's all bad and I *do* think he loves you. It occurs to me that you might try writing some of the scenes in your book from the parents' point of view. It should be challenging in both the professional and personal sense and probably useful, too.

Your chapter is powerful. Elspeth's anger feels very real. Keep sending your chapters to New York. I'll do my best to read them swiftly, but I feel confident in saying you don't need my chapter-to-chapter feedback in order to keep going. You're very surefooted.

Things are frantic here. I've been away so long and am so out of the habit of being the New York me that I can't seem to find my stride. I suppose it will all come back and I'll be glad when it does, though there are moments when I wonder. It doesn't help, of course, that I'm staying in a hotel. It's nice enough, but not very relaxing at the end of a long day. And I *hate* eating out. What was I ever thinking, subletting my apartment?

Could you do me an important favor? The tax information your father gave me was very useful. My taxes this year are so complex. Your father offered to look over my forms before I sent them in, but I hate to ask him. I know his department is under-staffed and your father is very busy. Do you think you could bring up the subject in a roundabout sort of way and sense whether he really has time to do it? I have an accountant, but he's such an unpleasant type—a cold, efficient fish—and I just can't face him.

Thanks, Liz. I hope all is well in Edgewood Heights.

Love,
Julia

Dear Journal,

I know I haven't been writing much lately, and when I do write it's not about truth and beauty or anything even slightly worth reporting. I'm sorry. There is a reason—there's nothing to write about. Julia said she liked my last chapter, but I could tell by the way she said it that it was the last thing on her mind. She's too busy with work and taxes (and needing my father to look them over—gag, gag, vomit). She's acting like Mrs. Reeves did at the end of last year, and while I don't blame people for having problems, it makes me feel left out. They're off in some world where I don't matter.

The only thing interesting that has happened is that I ran into Shana last week and she invited me to her beautiful apartment and started telling me all of these secrets about her life, which were pretty startling. Her husband cheats on her, which is a subject that makes me uncomfortable, but I'm flattered that she tells me. We're becoming friends and this is good. I can use a friend right now.

Dear Julia,

Thanks for reading my chapter when
you're so busy working. I've been busy too.
Mrs. Breiner (in English) is giving me extra
projects to "challenge" me. She's very nice
and is treating me like a friend. She wants
me to come to her house to see her first editions, and I might go. Also, I'm becoming
friends with Shana, Kelly's sister. She and
her husband are having problems and she
likes to talk to me. I can sympathize with the
problem of having to live with a thoughtless
man, since I've had lots of practice.

Speaking of which, I mentioned to Dad
you were grateful for the tax information
and he said he hoped you'd remember his
offer to help. So I guess he really means it.
But he's not a *tax* accountant, you know,
he's just a regular one who works for an
insurance company. Personally, I think you
should use a specialist. It seems to me a
cold, efficient fish is what you need for the

job. Though Dad is a bit cold and efficient himself, I guess.

I don't know about Dad's office being understaffed. He's always complaining about things like that, so I don't listen. He complains about everything. You wouldn't notice it at first, but after you've been around him for a while, it starts to bug you, fast. He's the opposite of you. When you complain about things, I can tell it's for a reason, and that you've put up with a lot before you even begin to complain.

I'd better go. I'm supposed to be at Shana's.

Love,

Liz

March 21, 1996

Dear Liz,

Thanks for your letter, though I must
say it made me sad. You sound so bitter
about your father. I know you don't want to
hear it, but I wish you two could make a little peace. Maybe your father has matured a
bit in the last few years and you haven't
noticed. What do you think? Try to look at
him with fresh eyes, as if the past hadn't
happened. What do you see? And that's all
I'll say about that.

I'm glad you're finding people to talk to,
though I'm not sure talking to a married
woman about marital problems will do you
much good. What about Kelly? Don't you
see her at all anymore?

Things are so trying here. Springtime was
recently bought out by a large conglomerate,
and despite promises to the contrary they're
inserting their fingers in every editorial pie.
I'm coasting along on nerves and don't have
much patience. Something has got to give.
I hope it's not me. Some mornings I just

can't stand to face the day.

Tell me what first editions you get to look at, if you do. Also, tell your dad I'm expressing the tax stuff to him and give him my heartfelt thanks. I'm sorry not to have gotten it to him sooner, but, as usual these days, I'm running wildly behind.

Love,
Julia

March 25, 1996

Dear Julia,

Yesterday I looked at my father with very fresh eyes. What did I see? A man who forgot it was my birthday. Of course when I came home from my mother's wearing her birthday gift, there was this mad scramble to wrap up some "birthday cash." I would have rather he just forget it than hand me a box full of money. It would have been more honest. More *mature*, if you know what I mean.

Your express package came and my father got right to work on it. I just hope that whatever my father tells you, you'll check it out with your cold, efficient fish. My father is not so perfect.

Love,
Liz

P.S. Talking to Shana about her problems does me a *lot* of good. It makes me feel

needed and helpful. And that's what friendship is all about, isn't it?—seeing your
friend's point of view and supporting her in
it. Kelly and I don't even talk. She's trying
out for cheerleading again and much too
busy for me.

Dear Liz,

I tried to call you twice tonight, as your
father will probably tell you. Your letter
upset me terribly.

First, my apologies for forgetting (not
knowing about!) your birthday myself. How
did it happen that in the course of our
friendship I never managed to ask about
your birthday? Anyway, I'm sorry. And I'm
sorry your father forgot. I know it hurt, but
he feels truly awful about it. It was only a
lapse in memory, it doesn't mean he doesn't
care.

I didn't mean to criticize your friendship
with Shana. You're a kind and thoughtful
girl, and I'm sure you're a comfort to her.
But surely a perceptive reader of Henry
James knows that friendship is *not* always
about supporting a friend in her point of
view. What if the friend makes a tragic mistake? Marital relationships, like all others,
are complex. One of these days Shana and
her husband may reunite, and Shana won't

forget it if you've disparaged her husband.
It's a difficult spot to maneuver, that's all I
meant. I've been burned in this regard
myself.

I need to talk to you and say these things
out loud. I need to clear the air between us.
Call me when you have a chance. I gave
your father both my work and home number
here. He tells me you aren't home much
these days. I assume you're at Shana's. Are
you at least finding time to enjoy the beautiful place?

Please, let's talk. I'll wait for you to call
me.

Love,
Julia

April 2, 1996

Dear Julia,

I know you want me to call, not write,
but I just don't feel like talking. I guess I'm
afraid of what I'll say. Or of what we'll say
to each other. I start to shake, literally, when
I think of it.

It doesn't matter that you didn't know
my birthday. I never told you when it was. I
don't know when yours is, either. I never
thought birthdays were all that important.
It's just that parents should remember, since
they give birth to you. It's supposed to be
one of the important moments in their lives.

It *does* matter that you talked this over
with my father. You talked *me* over with my
father. You told him something I said to you
in a letter, which was private.

I don't know about friendships and tragic
mistakes. I'm not analyzing my friendship
with Shana. What I do know is that she's
having a very bad time and I'm helping her
through it. I'll be amazed if she and her husband get back together, but if they do, so

what? Right now Shana needs me. She wants me to move in with her, and I'm thinking it over. I know Dad won't approve and you probably won't either, but I can't worry about that. I'm seventeen and it's time for me to make my own decisions.

Liz

April 5, 1996

Dear Liz—

Please call and talk to me. The tone of
your letter frightens me, it's so angry and
hurt. I need to talk to you. I won't force it by
calling you, but I will beg. Please Liz, call.

You're right, I do hate to think of your
moving out of your father's house. Seventeen
isn't as old as you think, though I'm the first
to admit how mature you are. I can't help
thinking you're moving because you're angry,
rather than because you're ready to go.

Your father and I didn't really discuss
you in the way you think. *He* told *me* that
you were angry because he forgot your
birthday. I would never reveal anything you
said to me in a letter.

If you called, we could discuss all of
this. I could make you understand. Please,
please, do.

Love,
Julia

April 10, 1996

Dear Liz—

I'm finding it very hard to keep my
promise not to call you. Your father called
me last night to tell me about your fight and
to say that you'd moved in with Shana. WE
DID NOT DISCUSS YOU. He was just
very, very worried and hopeful that I could
make you change your mind and come
home. I can't make you do anything and
told him so. I don't want to make you do
anything, except perhaps call me.

He gave me your number and address at
Shana's (with a minimum of words). I think
that if I haven't heard from you in a few
days, I'll call you there.

I love you, Liz. Being angry at your
father seems to have made you angry at me.
Why? We're not the same person.

Love,
Julia

Dear Journal,

How can a true friend not understand
why my being angry at my father has made
me angry at her, when she's taking his side?
No, they're not the same person, but now
they're linked, and she's supposed to be
linked with *me*. Maybe I don't hate her, the
way I hate my father, but this huge mountain of disappointment rises up whenever I
think of her. Shana says it's sort of like
knowing that her husband is with another
woman when he should be here with her—
she feels sick inside and totally lonely. It's
good I'm with Shana. We help each other.

But Journal, I cry a lot.

Dear Liz,

I do get the message. Shana was rude, I
must say, but I suppose she sees it as friendship. It isn't friendship, to cut you off from
people who love you, but I'm going to stop
telling you such things. It's why you resent
me, of course.

I'm sorry for whatever pain I've caused
you. I'm sorry about lots of things. Reading
back over your letters, I see very clearly how
many mistakes I've made. How stupid of me
not to understand that you would resent a
friendship between me and your father. I
saw the friendship as minor—as a reflection
of my interest in you—so it never occurred
to me that it might seriously hurt you.

I think my major error has been in forgetting the age gap between us. You're such
a precocious girl in so many ways that I've
often thought of you as an equal. I'm a
strong believer in mending fences with our
parents and making peace with our pasts;
but you're still living your past. I think I

became aware of this when I met you and your father, and I sort of shifted gears—started giving motherly advice. How absurd. It wasn't what you wanted or what you needed.

It seems to me I've made so many mistakes lately. Maybe in a way I did reach out towards your father a little, without even knowing it. He's so anchored in everyday life while I've let so much slip that now I have nowhere solid to stand. Certainly I reached out to you, and maybe unfairly. You needed an editor and I drew you into a friendship simply because you're so like the girl I was and would like, still, to be. And, of course, I was lonely. It was more than unfair, I think, it was maybe even abusive. Oh Liz, please forgive me. And please go on writing your book. You haven't needed me for any of it.

I've valued our friendship more than you'll ever know. You mustn't ever feel remorse about anything. The mistakes were all mine.

Love always,

Julia

Dear Journal of a "Precocious Girl,"

That's what Julia called me—a girl. And she's valued our friendship more than I'll ever know, even though it wasn't between "equals." It's also clearly over. Dear Journal, I cried for more than an hour when I got that letter. Was I crying because I was mad and insulted and hurt or because I realized I'm going to miss Julia so much that I can hardly stand it? I don't honestly know. Yes, I was angry, but I think part of me believed Julia would keep calling and begging forever. Now she's stopped, and Journal—what will I do without her?

4/19/96

Dear Journal,

You will not believe this. Shana's husband came over tonight and they went into the bedroom and I think they slept together. After all the hours of my hearing her say how she'll never ever forgive him and of trying to help her get on with her life, all Paul had to do was show up once. Where is her self-respect? It's just what Julia said would happen.

Life is so weird. My father calls every night now and just acts nice. He doesn't pressure me to come home or anything, he says he's only "checking in." But he sounds pretty lonely and I have to think: how pathetic that I'm what kept him from being lonely when we never even talked.

4/22/96

Weirder and Weirder, Dear Journal—

Today at school Mr. Grisham came up to me in the hall and told me he'd been sorry to lose me this year! He looked like he meant it, too. JUST LIKE JULIA SAID. (How many times will I have to write these words??) I was totally speechless and stuttered something back.

Then, as if that were not enough weirdness for just one day, Kelly came over here after school and, when Shana was in the kitchen, looked at me really funny, looked around the room, then told me that she felt jealous—not of my having her sister, but of her sister's having me! Speechless again. Kelly finally had to laugh because of how shocked I looked, but then Shana came back in the room and we couldn't finish the conversation. The part we had sure made me happy, though. Happy and confused. I went to bed wondering: why don't I really like living in this apartment, even though it's so perfect? The answer was: because I miss my own life. (!!!) Yes, dear Journal, I actually miss my room in our ugly split-down-the-middle house. I miss writing my letters to Julia on my clunky old wooden desk, which Kelly and I ruined in the first grade when we carved all the words we could spell into it. (Needless to say, I ruined it the most.) I even miss my dad. Explain *that* to my old self. Explain my new self to my old self!

Dear Journal of a Definitely *Not* Precocious
Girl,

I was so insulted when Julia called me a
girl in her last letter. In fact, I hated her for
it. But now I think, I *am* a girl. I don't
understand anything about the world. I certainly don't understand Shana. She spends
all day crying and saying she hates her husband, and then he comes over and she
sleeps with him. I know this for a fact
because she admitted it.

And my father keeps calling and being
nice. He says he wants to talk—*really* talk,
in a grown-up–to–grown-up manner. The
amazing thing is I think he means it. I can't
bring myself to actually do it yet, but I feel
like I'm getting close. Sometimes he seems
more like the person that Julia was talking
about than the one I've known all my life.
He says he's been thinking about my mother
and where they went wrong and how he
never used to listen. This is true rational
thought! Of course he can't make it through
a whole phone call. Just when I start to like

him, he says something annoying. Still, it means a lot that he's trying so hard.

Everything seems more complicated than it used to, dear Journal, and not just good or bad. So now I have to wonder: what good does it do a person to get older and wiser if, the wiser she gets, the more she will understand that nothing is ever simple??

Dear Journal of the Idiot Who Used to Be
Angry at Mrs. Reeves—

—who came into school today and
brought her baby girl. Oh, dear Journal, she
was so adorable you wouldn't believe it.
Mrs. Reeves tracked me down specifically
and asked how my writing was going. I said
"fine" and hurried to change the subject,
which wasn't hard with that wiggly little
baby wanting our attention.

Mrs. Reeves is the perfect adoring mother.
She told me she'd been so worried before
that she wouldn't be—that she'd been
depressed when she found out she was preg-
nant and had spent the last few months of
the school year last year trying to make the
decision to take a break from teaching and
really enjoy her baby. I have to ask myself:
how many things and people did I just not
SEE last year? I knew Mrs. Reeves was
unhappy for some reason, but I never seriously stopped to wonder why. I only worried
that she wasn't thinking of *me*. Dear Journal,
you will not believe what Mrs. Reeves said

when she was leaving—that she hopes her baby grows into a person as fine and as special as ME. I felt so unworthy I almost cried.

I've been so stupid about everything, especially Julia. Things didn't have to just stop—that was my own decision, which I made by not writing back or answering her phone calls. My pride was hurt so I wanted to punish her. What a total jerk.

May 7, 1996

Dear Julia,

I'm sorry. For not answering your phone calls and for not answering your letter much sooner than this. I felt so rotten hearing Shana be rude to you, but I just couldn't talk. I needed time to think about what had happened.

It seems to me now that not much did happen. I was being pretty childish. You were so kind to me, of course you'd be kind to my father too. And if I didn't like it, I should have just told you right out. We could have talked it over. I *was* confusing anger at my father with anger at you. I couldn't stand the thought that you might take his side against me or end up liking him more than you like me. I was jealous, so I tried to make you jealous of Shana. (And even of Mrs. Breiner!) The fault was *not* all yours. It was mine, too. Even mostly mine.

To tell the truth, it hasn't been that great, living in Shana's apartment. All Shana does is cry and then sleep with her husband if he chooses to show up. I think you're right—in the end they're going to get back together. When that happens, I'll have to move out. She doesn't see me as some great friend, just someone to fill the space.

Now I can't bear the cold bright light that pours through Shana's windows. It makes me feel empty and alone. How's that for irony?

I wish there could be friendships that just *were*, that went on and on, no matter what. Marriages are supposed to be like that, but no one's ever is, as far as I can see. I think that my friendship with you was the best one I've ever had or ever will have. I can't believe I spoiled it. I don't see why differences in age should matter, if people relate soul to soul. I honestly think we did. You said yourself that we're alike.

I hope we can start over. Please write soon. I'd say call, but Shana is always here and I probably couldn't talk. And I'm too embarrassed to call you.

Love,
Liz

Springtime Press
One East 56th Street
New York, NY 10022
May 17, 1996

Ms. Elizabeth Beech
51 Cunningham Street, Apt. 4A
Edgewood Heights, NJ 08025

Dear Ms. Beech:

I'm returning your letter to Julia Steward Jones. As it was marked "personal," we didn't feel we should open it. Ms. Jones is no longer with us. She asked that her mail be forwarded to Virginia, but as it comes back from there forwarded to us, we've stopped doing so.

We gather you're a friend. If you locate Ms. Jones, would you ask her to send us a new address? And please, pass on our best wishes.

Sincerely,
Lorraine Bridgeman
Editorial Assistant

51 Cunningham Street,
Apt. 4A
Edgewood Heights, NJ 08025
May 20, 1996

Ms. Lorraine Bridgeman
Springtime Press
One East 56th St.
New York, NY 10022

Dear Ms. Bridgeman,

I have no idea where Julia Steward Jones
is, but I'm very, very worried. She didn't tell
me she'd be leaving, and yes, we're good
friends. When did she leave, and why?
Someone must know where she is. What
about the person who sublets her apartment?

Please write or call me as soon as possible. My phone number is (609) 555–7168.

Sincerely,
Elizabeth Beech

Dear Journal,

Julia isn't working at Springtime Press
and she isn't in Virginia—I know because I
tried calling and her phone is disconnected.
So where *is* she?? I have this awful sinking
feeling in the bottom of my stomach. I don't
know what it means. Or what anything
means. I'm not writing about my problems
with Shana or my father or anything else,
because compared to the thought of a missing
Julia, what problem is worth the words?

Springtime Press
One East 56th Street
New York, NY 10022
June 7, 1996

Ms. Elizabeth Beech
51 Cunningham Street, Apt. 4A
Edgewood Heights, NJ 08025

Dear Ms. Beech:

Thank you for writing. Ms. Jones left Springtime Press on April 22 for reasons I'm not free to divulge. As I think I mentioned in my last letter, she requested that we forward her mail to Virginia; however, that mail comes back to us and we have no further address. The person in her apartment doesn't know where she is, but we all assume she'll be back soon, as she left personal effects in the office. When she turns up, we'll inform her of your inquiries. In the meantime, if you hear from her first, please let us know.

Sincerely,
Lorraine Bridgeman
Editorial Assistant

Dear Journal,

    I think I've lost Julia! I've lost her by being selfish and childish and stupid. By only thinking of me. Julia once told me to try and tell my story from my parents' point of view, and I didn't know why. Now I do. She wanted me to really see things instead of just thinking of how they look to *me*. It probably seems like I'm thinking only of ME right this minute when I should be worrying about Julia, but the thing is, Julia's not really missing—she's only missing from me and from a job she hated. Julia ran away, and Journal, I don't blame her.

Dear Julia,

I guess it's foolish to write you a letter
when I don't know where to send it, but I
need to talk to you so much. I need to tell
you how sorry I am about things and how
much I care. I feel like such a fool. Last
night I read over every one of your letters
and it's all so clear—you were miserable and
I didn't really *see*. I try to remember what
things I wrote back to you. All I remember
thinking about is me—my problems at
school and my problems at home and my
problems with writing. You were losing your
parents and your childhood home and
maybe even your job and trying to share
your loss with me. I was worrying about Mr.
Grisham's picking on me in class. Can you
ever, ever forgive me?

I guess you've sold your parents' house.
That must have been so hard on you. I like
to think that you're off on a cruise somewhere, having a vacation from all the decisions and the people (i.e., me) who've been

driving you nuts. At first I got panicky when I realized I didn't have *any* address for you, but then I thought, "Julia's going to come back—she'll come when she's ready!" and it just felt true. When you do, I'll show you the letters I've written in your absence and you'll see how much I care.

Julia, I love you always, with all my heart.

Liz

Dear Journal of a Wimp Who's Going
Home,

Yep, dear Journal, I caved. It's all very
weird. Tonight I was talking to Dad on the
phone and he mentioned my birthday for the
four hundredth time and I suddenly realized—he doesn't even *know* why I've been
angry all this time! He thinks I moved out
because he forgot my birthday. It seemed so
pathetic. I remembered what Julia said about
his being lonely, and I decided she was right.
Who really talks to Dad? No one, I guess.
Before, he was not a person you could talk
to. But maybe neither was I. I know we'll
still fight and drive each other crazy, but
even that seems more right than my being
here. Shana is driving me up the wall. I
think Paul's coming back. When I try to
remind her of some of his faults and the rotten things he's done, she gets mad at *me*, just
like Julia said she would. I cannot wait to get
out of this place. (No comment needed.)

June 11, 1996

Dear Julia,

Guess what? I'm going home! I'm even a
little happy about it, in a peculiar sort of
way. Isn't that strange? But no, to you it's
probably not, since you didn't think I should
leave in the first place. I wish I could talk to
you, Julia, and tell you how right you were
about so many things.

Julia, where are you? I'm not religious,
but last night I said a prayer that I'd hear
from you soon. Then I closed my eyes and
pictured you on a cruise, relaxing in the sun.
There you were in a deck chair, forgetting
your problems (even *me*, which was all right
if it made you feel happy again). But at the
end of the cruise, when you were feeling
peaceful and fine, you had this sudden urge
to call me. And you did. It helped me fall
asleep.

Love,
Liz

146 West Cliff Street
Edgewood Heights, NJ 08025
June 11, 1996

Ms. Lorraine Bridgeman
Springtime Press
One East 56th Street
New York, NY 10022

Dear Ms. Bridgeman,

Thank you for your letter. I think Julia Jones is probably just taking a vacation. I'll let you know if I hear from her. If you get her new address first, could you send it to me right away? I know she wouldn't mind.

Very sincerely,
Elizabeth Beech

P.S. Please notice my address has changed.

Dear Journal of a Person Who's Back in Her Room Again—

—and feeling very odd. This is home but not home. Dad took time off from work to help me move (yes, I did say time off from work!), and even Mom came over and carried some things in from the car when she saw us unloading boxes. She and Dad spent one whole hour in each other's presence with only minor shouting. Whenever they'd start to get mad, they'd look at me and clamp their mouths closed, then we'd smile these phony smiles. "Are we rehearsing a *Brady Bunch* show?" I asked them once, but nobody laughed.

After Mom left, Dad asked me how Julia was and I realized he didn't *know*. Instead of feeling angry at his interest, I just felt relieved to tell someone that she was missing. And when he looked upset, I didn't feel one twinge of jealousy, only gratefulness that he cared. He said if I wanted him to, he would call Springtime Press and ask some more questions, since sometimes adults can get information that teenagers can't. I begged him to do it, even though before I would have been annoyed at his interference and at his implying that I'm a child. It's like I'm happy to be a child again for a little while and have someone help me to make decisions. (!!) Is this a bad thing or a good one? Julia could answer the question.

Anyway, tonight I'm too tired to think, so good night, dear Journal. How does it feel to be back on the desk of your childhood?

June 13, 1996

Dear Julia,

Okay, now I'm worried. Dad called
Springtime today and found out that the tax
information he expressed back to you was
still in New York with your mail. That
means you didn't file taxes. He says responsible people like you don't ignore taxes even
if they're a little late with them.

I don't know. I like to think that you're
taking a break from life and taxes, but I have
to admit it alarmed me when I figured out
that no one has heard from you since April
22nd—that's 52 days, a pretty long cruise.
Dad suggested we call the New York police.
This seems rather extreme to me, and I told
him you'd resent it. The editors at Springtime agree with him though. I refuse to
believe anything bad has happened to you.
You're out there, I know you are, and whatever you're doing is just what you need
to do.

It's been really hard to concentrate on
my paper for Mrs. Breiner, but I think it's

done. It's a pretty impressive paper (over seven pages long) on flower imagery in *The Portrait of a Lady*. Someday I hope you'll read it. I haven't worked on my novel for two months now. There's been too much confusing emotion and change going on. You'd probably tell me to *use* the emotion, but right now I can't and I don't even really want to. Or no, that's not true—I do want to, but when I sit down to write about Elspeth, I only think about you.

Julia, write to me. Please.

Love,
Liz

June 16, 1996

Dear Julia,

This has been such a confusing day. I
don't know if I can write about all the things
tangled up in my head. It's not that much
has happened, it's just that since I've been
home, I keep seeing things with slightly different eyes, and it's startling all the time.
Everything has to be rethought, you know?

Mom and Dad, for instance. Mom came
over after dinner for some fighting time with
Dad. Watching them, it occurred to me that
Mom sort of likes to fight. It's her way of
talking. And it's not always really fighting,
either. She's trying to be heard. Dad doesn't
listen to her enough. It's funny, Kelly used
to tell me my mom wasn't yelling when I'd
say she was. Today I realized she wasn't literally yelling when it seemed like she was.
It's a tone of voice thing that was threatening when I was a child. It *felt* like yelling.

So suddenly the way I think about my
parents and about Kelly and about you shifted
just a bit. And it seemed as if things could

go on shifting forever and ever, so that just when I think I know some truth, it will start to be something different. Which made me wonder—what does a writer write about if there's no "right" way of seeing?

I'll never sleep tonight, Julia. If you were here, you could help me understand things. Your letters were always so clear and full of good advice, even if I didn't always want to hear it. Every day I hope I'll find one of those letters in the mailbox. But I don't. Will I, soon? Will I ever? The answer has to be yes. Please, let it be yes.

Love,
Liz

Dear Journal,

Explain things to me. Tell me what I'm "seeing" this time. Tonight my mother came over, and, somehow, Julia's name came up in the conversation. Mom heard how Dad has been calling New York and calling the house in Virginia and generally going nuts looking for her. For instance, today he called the phone company in Va. to find out when her phone was disconnected. They told him that was confidential information. Anyway, Mom told Dad he was being his usual obsessive self and Dad said how can you *not* obsess about someone who disappears from the face of the earth? Mom said, "Easy, unless you love that person."

Dad stormed out of the room, but it made me stop and think. Does Dad LOVE Julia? Holy cow. As jealous as I was, this never occurred to me. Not that he had real, true feelings about her as a person. I tried to ask him about it later, but he just looked furious. He said Mom was being her usual garbage-minded self and that not everything had to be reduced to *Enquirer* newspaper trivia. Fairly poetic thinking for Dad. Maybe he really did write Julia a charming, witty letter. Suddenly I felt like I hardly know him. (Which happens a LOT lately.)

Anyway, now I do have to wonder: why *is* Dad going overboard looking for Julia? I can understand why *I* would do it, but he hardly knows her. What does his interest mean? It's not the kind of interest the old Dad would have shown in any woman he didn't have "plans" for. And if he does love Julia, how do I feel about it? Besides confused.

Journal, I don't have a clue. But then, the list of things I don't have a clue about lately would fill a million journals, so what else is new?

June 17, 1996

Dear Julia,

A very odd but interesting fight went on
in this house tonight (I'll spare you the gory
details), and I've been sitting in my room
ever since trying to "look with fresh eyes" at
the facts and figure out what's happening.
It's hard, though. I can't separate out what I
might be imagining from what I'm actually
seeing. Have you ever noticed how once an
idea gets into your head, you can start to
interpret everything around it? Then, if you
put a different spin on the same idea, you
can come up with an opposite conclusion
even though the facts haven't changed. It's
like wearing some weird glasses that make
the world look one way if you stare straight
ahead and another if you turn sideways, and
on and on. How can a person know which
vision is the truth? And don't you have to,
to be a writer? I don't think I'll ever be one.

I handed in my paper today. Mrs.
Breiner read half of it while I was standing
there and said it was college-level work. It

made me decide for sure that I want to apply to college. Dad said he'd take me around this summer to look at places and help me find scholarships to apply for. He seems proud that I might go. All this is thanks to you, Julia. But now come back and advise me. I'm fantasizing about the University of Virginia, but I suspect Dad will say it's too far to go and too expensive for a non-Virginia resident, not to mention too hard to get into. He's talking about Rutgers or Trenton State. Everyone from around here goes to those schools, though, and it would just be more of the same. Or would it? They're both good colleges. Help, Julia! I know you'd know the very place I should go.

Dad has talked to police in New York City and made you an official missing person. I keep thinking of what you'll say when you step off that cruise ship and find out police are hunting for you. The police seem to agree with Dad about the tax forms and the fact that you left all your stuff at work. I don't. I remember how hard it was for you to deal with sorting through your parents' things in Virginia and how much you were dreading the mess on your desk. I think you just got tired of it all and finally ran away. Dad looks relieved but not totally convinced whenever I say this, and I guess I'm not totally convinced either. You've started to *feel* far away. Oh, Julia, don't really be lost. I couldn't bear it.

Love,
Liz

Dear Journal,

Do you know what? I think maybe Dad does love Julia. Or at least feels attached in some way. God! I don't know what to do with this idea. I can't blame him, of course. It would be the first smart thing he's ever done when it comes to women! And I refuse to get jealous, ever. It's a stupid, petty emotion. Still, I feel a funny knot in my stomach and my mind goes kind of blank when I try to really picture it: Dad and Julia. I don't know *how* to understand it, if you know what I mean.

I need Julia to come back here and help me deal with all of this. Journal, where is she?

Dear Julia,

I tried to write tonight. I got to thinking about Elspeth and how I left her fuming at her dad and Patsy and enjoying her mother's tricks. I decided I'd make her mother do something so awful that Elspeth would have to feel sympathy for her father and Patsy— to see their point of view at least a little.

It didn't work. Every sentence I wrote felt stupid, like it was just some game, and I wanted to rip the whole book up. I couldn't, though—it would have been like murdering Elspeth, and I do still believe in her. I think she needs Julia. You see, it *isn't* true that I could have written this book without you. I don't think I can write anything else, either, which makes me scared. If I'm not a writer, what am I, Julia?

Love,
Liz

Dear Journal,

Dad and I had a long, long talk about Julia tonight. It was the first time we've ever really talked completely honestly about something that mattered. It was amazing. Ever since, I've been trying to decide whether I really was misreading him all this time, the way Julia said, or whether he's matured and changed. Maybe both. And I've matured too. Some of the things that bugged me about him (and still bug me!) don't seem all that important now.

I told Dad about the rotten things I said to Julia in the last letter I sent her and how ashamed I was of it—how the stupid jealousy seemed pretty childish now. I must confess I was telling Dad partly because I wanted to hear what he'd say about his feelings for Julia.

Dad looked sort of shocked and was quiet for a minute. Then he said he supposed my jealousy wasn't all that outrageous since he really was sort of interested in Julia, even though he didn't tell her or maybe even admit it to himself. He said she was different from other women he's known—that she seemed serious and honest and like someone who didn't play games, which is why he thinks she's really missing. He said he'd never met a person like her, and I agreed with that.

Most amazing of all, though, is that he said he was mainly interested in her because she was close to me and *he* was jealous of that! So that I was right, in a way, to be annoyed, because he *was* trying to butt in. I thought it was unbelievable that he admitted this. It's so sad to think how love can get all twisted around like that.

But also he was interested in Julia in a kind of nice simple way after he got to know her. He said he couldn't imagine any professional giving so much time to a teenager for an unselfish reason. It fascinated him and made him feel happy that she was helping me, even when he was jealous of it. He said that when he cooked her dinner and drove her back to the city, he felt like he was sort of taking care of my guardian angel and making up for some of the unhappiness he'd caused

278

in my life. Coming from Dad, this was all incredible—almost like poetry.

Journal, will I ever sleep again? Each night when I go to bed there's something new that keeps me awake.

6/20/96

Dear Journal,

I woke up today thinking yesterday was a dream—had my father really said all that? Had we really talked to each other like human beings? Yes, we had. And we went right on doing it through the big dinner Dad decided to cook tonight, for some unknown reason.

He told me something I'd never have believed in a million years until this week. He said the reason he'd stayed in this house with my mother was because he thought if he did, we would still be a kind of family and that was important to him. (!) He didn't have a family when he was growing up. His mother died when he was born, so it was only Dad and his dad. Sad, huh? I'd never thought about that, even though I knew it.

He was also afraid that if he moved out, I'd go and live with my mother. It hurt him that my brother Roger never came to visit our side of the house except when he had to. My brother is just like that—he hasn't come back from California since he left a year ago. But to my father it was a real true hurt. He thought I might be the same. And he said he guessed that was why he didn't like for me to travel. He didn't want to lose me. Journal, I never saw this, ever, in all the years I lived here. But I believe that it's true. It's also true that he might have lost me too, because we didn't know each other, the way none of us know Roger.

Anyway, we talked about how hard it is to really understand what another person is thinking and how people do misread each other. This made me think of Julia's last letter and how things got so confused. I went and got that letter and showed it to Dad. I couldn't believe I did it, after how angry I'd gotten that Julia had even discussed me with him. Now here I was showing him the most personal of her letters! I thought she would understand and approve, though. It was as if she were bringing the two of us closer, which was what she wanted.

That letter really scared my father. He said it read like a farewell note. I pointed out that it *was* a farewell note, since it was the last one Julia planned to write me, but he said no, a real farewell note. I guess he meant the suicide kind. He suddenly got very nervous and started grabbing plates off the table and banging around in the kitchen.

I refuse to believe my father, absolutely refuse. Julia is a life-giving kind of person and she's out there, alive.

Isn't she, Journal?

Dear Julia,

Please come back. I want to tell you all
the amazing things that are going on in my
life. Dad and I are actually communicating.
We still annoy each other, but now when it
happens we talk about it instead of just shutting each other out.

Things are better with Kelly also. She
came over today after school to talk to
me about Shana. She agrees with me that
Shana did a dumb thing by taking her husband back, and she wanted to hear about
what I knew from living over there. I tried
to tell her enough to be helpful, but I also
tried not to violate anything Shana told
me in confidence. Even though Shana and
I aren't friends anymore, we were friends
then, when she confided in me, and I
respect that.

I started thinking about how relationships
are always changing, as if they were living
things. Kelly and I discussed this and it was

nice, one of the best talks we've ever had. Kelly seems to have matured a little too. She isn't very rah-rah cheerleader at the moment and she really listened to what I was saying, which she doesn't usually do. It was so nice, having a friend again. Kelly told me that lots of people would like to be my friend, but they always think I'm not interested because I keep apart. I told her I keep apart because I feel apart and thought no one cared. We ended up laughing at the general dumbness of life. She invited me to go to Maine with her this summer. I told her I couldn't because I can't go anywhere until Dad finds you, plus the college hunt is on, and I'll be working again part-time. But I was really happy she asked me.

Julia, everything good that's happening is all thanks to you. You taught me to be more open-minded (even though it took me a while to learn!) and to think about people in a *real* way, instead of just how they affect me. You change people and things. You're changing us now, without even being here. Dad called you my guardian angel, and I

think he was right. But who's guarding you?
You are, I guess. I believe you can handle
anything. I love you—

Liz

Dear Julia,

Hope! Dad and I both felt it today. This morning he called the police in New York City to see if anything new had happened, and while it hasn't, really, they did find out some information that changes the whole picture. They asked the editors at Springtime to go through everything on your desk and look for clues to where you might be. No clues turned up, but people started noticing some things were missing. Most importantly, for me, the bookends that I gave you. You brought them to New York from Virginia, then took them away when you left.

Everyone is relieved—Dad and the police because you're probably out there, alive (as *I've* known all along), and me because you still cared enough and forgave me enough to take those bookends with you. I feel oddly sad and happy at the same time, thinking about this.

Dad has found out about your being sort of fired from your job. I'm so, so sorry. I know you didn't feel like doing that job right now, but I'm sure you cared about it. You are such a wonderful editor.

Dad says you must have been very depressed and that that's why you left your taxes and all the other stuff behind. He thinks you're in some hospital or clinic. It seems possible to me, though I hate to think about it. But it's equally possible what I thought before—that you just gave it all up and went off on a cruise or some other interesting trip without really caring. Either way, the police aren't much interested anymore. Dad said he would call every hospital and clinic in New York City, then New York State, then the whole east coast until he found you. He put his hand on my shoulder in this "don't worry, honey, I'm in control" way that was both amusing and sort of touching.

Now he's off making phone calls. Part of me wants desperately for him to find you, of course, but the other part is afraid. What would it mean if you've been in a clinic all this time? Would they have locked you up? I started to ask Dad but couldn't bring myself to do it. I was too afraid of the answer.

.It's late. Good night, Julia. Sweet
dreams, wherever you are. (When I was little, my mother used to say "sweet dreams"
to me every night. I reminded her of that the
other day and she actually started crying! Is
the whole world going crazy?)

Love,

Liz

Dear Journal,

I can't believe it! Dad has actually found Julia and she *is* in a clinic, one in North Jersey. It doesn't seem real, I've gotten so used to not knowing. She'd become a sort of person in my head or that hovering guardian angel, just out of sight, but always there.

Now we're wondering what we should do. Will she want to hear from me? See me? Hate me (us!) for tracking her down? Dad says that tomorrow her doctor is going to call and give him advice. People at the clinic told Dad that no one has come to see Julia in all this time. Isn't that the saddest?

Oh, Journal, I hope Julia's all right. She can't be happy, locked up in some clinic. Dad says it's an excellent place and that I shouldn't think of it as "locked up," since Julia signed herself in. But it isn't exactly a cruise, is it? Or maybe, in a way, it is. I remember what she said about depression and the mind needing a rest. Maybe that's all she's doing—giving herself a rest.

Dear Journal,

Dad talked to Julia's doctor today. He wouldn't tell us details about what happened to her, and I guess he shouldn't. Dad says psychiatrists can't betray their patients' confidences. Plus we're not her family. But since there isn't any family, he did agree to tell Dad the basics: that she had a nervous breakdown and that she came to the clinic from a hospital in New York, where they felt she should get away from the city. Oh, Journal, Julia was in some big, cold hospital, all alone. It breaks my heart. And I can't help thinking that I'm to blame. I was so, so cruel to her. I'll never forgive myself.

Dad's furious that the New York police didn't find her there. He said if they had, we could have seen her and helped her sooner. I don't know why he's so sure we're going to be a help. I'm hardly her best friend at the moment, and Dad is almost a stranger. When I pointed this out to him, he got angry. He said we both had a "connection" with Julia that was bigger than everyday life and that she understood that. This is a little over the top, if you ask me, and pretty cosmic stuff— nothing at all like Dad. Or maybe it is. I'm trying to accept that Dad is a person I can't fully know, like every other person.

The doctor is going to talk to Julia about us and call Dad back. I'm so nervous. Will she want to hear from us? Say yes, Julia, please.

6/25/96

Dear Journal,

Today Dad talked to Julia's doctor for 45 minutes. I don't know exactly what he said, since Dad gave him his number at work (a rotten trick), and the information is coming to me in bits and pieces scattered around Dad's theories of psychotherapy and his rantings about police. Here's what I know so far:

Julia was amazed to hear we had searched for her, and she does want to see us—oh, thank you, God, thank you—but not quite yet. According to the doctor, she's still a little unsteady, but she's much, much better (better than *what* I do not know), and will be back to "normal" soon. He said she experienced too many losses at once—first her parents and then her job. He didn't mention friendships, or Dad didn't tell me if he did, but I'm sure it was implied. Journal, even I'm not egotistical enough to think I was as important to Julia as her parents or her job, but I know I was a loss. Or at least a big disappointment. I let Julia down when she needed me the most.

The doctor suggested we write Julia a letter as a "gentle first step" back into her life. Ironic, right?—as if letters are never upsetting. Well, hopefully mine won't be, ever again.

But Journal, what should a "gentle" letter say?

June 25, 1996

Dear Julia,

I'm not going to write you a long letter
until you write back and tell me you want
me to. I'll just say that I love you and miss
you and am so, so sorry. Everything good
that has happened to me has been thanks
to you, and I caused you nothing but pain. I
hope you can someday forgive me, but for
now all that matters is that you're okay. We
were so scared when we couldn't find you.

I love you, Julia.

Liz

June 28, 1996

Dear Liz,

How could you possibly doubt that I'd
want to hear from you? I'd like nothing
more right now than to have one of your
lively letters.

I'm astonished you and your Dad managed to find me here. I'm sorry that I scared
you. I should have thought to tell someone
where I was. But of course I wasn't really
thinking.

There's nothing to forgive, Liz. You did
not cause me only pain, you caused me a
great deal of happiness. Please write to me
soon.

Love,
Julia

Dear Journal of a Person Too Happy to
Live—

Julia forgives me! She says there's nothing *to* forgive, which of course is a lie, but I
can tell it's how she feels, if not what she
knows is true. And her letter sounded normal, just like the old Julia's. Dad said the
doctor thinks we may be able to see her very
soon.

Oh, Journal, I must be the luckiest person on earth. Today, when the kids at the
day-care center spun me around to make me
dizzy, I laughed so hard that I couldn't
speak and then *everyone* started laughing and
the whole school was happy for the rest of
the day. I loved being Dizzy Lizzy (even the
teachers call me that now)—like some
happy, contagious disease.

July 2, 1996

Dear Julia,

I was so relieved to get your letter. Dad
and I were worried you might be upset that
we tracked you down. We couldn't help it,
though, when we heard no one knew where
you were. For Dad it was the unmailed tax
forms that were the most alarming. In his
world no one neglects taxes!

I'm so sorry to hear about what has happened to you. I don't exactly *know*, of
course, but I know you must have suffered a
lot. One of the awful things for me after you
disappeared, besides, of course, not knowing
if you were okay, was not being able to tell
you how right you were about everything
and how wrong I was. I wrote to say I was
sorry, but the letter came back from
Springtime. That's how we found out you
were missing. The thought that you were
gone and I couldn't ever apologize was the
worst thing I've ever felt.

I've been writing to you anyway. Someday I'll show you the letters when you feel

ready, and you'll see how much I missed
you and how guilty I've felt. I still can't
believe it—after all you did for me, I wasn't
there when you needed me.

So much has changed for me, Julia—all of
it good—and it's all because of you. Dad and
I are friends! Every day we talk about something real. We're actually a lot alike. Can you
believe I'd ever say *that*?! It was talking about
you that helped us to learn to know each
other in the first place. Dad said he envied
me having my writing—something I really
love—and someone to talk to about it. He
hasn't had any true interest since he's been a
grown-up. When he was young he loved lots
of things—sports, and fishing, and nature,
and camping *alone* in the woods. I guess mar-
rying Mom spoiled all that. Plus having to
make money. Part of the reason he works so
hard is because we do need the money. He
helps my grandfather pay his bills, which I
never knew. His life doesn't have any magic, I
have to admit it. I told him he should start
reading. He looked at me like I was crazy, but
he didn't say no! Anyway, we keep having
these great discussions and one always leads

to another. It's as if we're catching up on a lifetime of never talking.

Things are better with Mom, also. She has a boyfriend at the moment, so she's too busy to fight. Really though, she doesn't seem to want to fight much anymore. She looks at us with her big wild eyes, then just sighs and smiles. I feel like I'm living in some weird parallel universe. It probably won't last, but it also won't ever be like it was, I know that.

You were right about so many things, Julia, and I want to talk to you about all of them. I hope you and I can start over when you feel well enough.

Love always,
Liz

July 5, 1996

Dear Liz,

The last thing I want is for you to feel
guilty. Nothing that happened to me was
your fault. I wasn't right and you weren't
wrong. We were just looking at life from different perspectives for a while.

I'm glad you and your dad are friends
and glad to think I might have had something to do with it. You changed my life too,
Liz. You reminded me of much that I had
lost in myself. It's easy, when you grow
older, to let the fine things slip away.
Someday, when we're together, I want to
talk to you about what I've been through. It
hasn't been only bad, Liz. In fact, in the
end, it's been good.

Guess what? I've started writing, an old
dream of mine. I'm not particularly good at
it, I think, but that doesn't stop me. There's
no one here to judge. Really, there's no one
anywhere to judge, when you think about it.
No one who matters. When it comes right
down to it, we only matter to ourselves and

to the people who love us, and since I'm short, at the moment, on people who love me, I feel astonishingly free to do and say and write whatever I please.

Here's a working version of a poem I've been writing. It's not much good as poetry, but it says something I haven't found other words to say. What do you think? You can judge. You're one who loves me.

> I forgot the morning sun
> It caught my moon ascended
> And saw my fears strung through the sky
> From star to star
> Like lullabies
> Or stories without endings
>
> But suddenly I saw the wind
> Rise up
> They fluttered free
> To float upon the air in utter peace
> And in that gentle flap
> Give birth to me

And what about *your* writing? I can't

wait to hear what Elspeth has been up to. Send me whatever you've done, and send the letters you wrote me, if you feel ready for me to see them. I'm hungry for writer's talk. You don't know the meaning of "parallel universe" until you've spent weeks talking to doctors! (But of course, they've helped me and I'm truly grateful.)

Give my best to your father and write again soon.

Love,
Julia

Dear Julia,

I can't believe you wrote that beautiful
poem and that you shared it with *me*. I've
read it over and over, trying to understand
it. Maybe it isn't right to analyze someone's
poetry, but I can't help wanting to know
what it says since everything you've ever said
has been important to me. I hope you don't
mind.

I didn't understand it at first, but suddenly it was there, perfectly clear. When you
had your breakdown, all of your fears were
exposed—strung up for the world to see. But
their exposure also set them free, or set you
free of them, so you could finally be the person you always wanted to be.

I love the image of the fears strung "star
to star/Like lullabies/Or stories without endings." I don't know if I can say what the
image means, but I can feel it, which is the
point of images, I guess. Lullabies do express
and soothe our fears as they swing and sing
(strung star to star!) through the night. I'm

not sure about "stories without endings," except that it's mysterious, like life, I guess. I decided, when I wrote my paper on *The Portrait of a Lady*, that the reader isn't supposed to really know in the end what happens to Isabel Archer. Yes, she goes back to her husband in Italy, but is she going back to leave him, or going back to stay? There can't ever be an ending to a story, can there? Even death doesn't end things. If you had never come back to my father and me, you'd go on changing our lives anyway. Everywhere you look, there are stories without endings.

Which is why, I guess, I can't write. I haven't in ages. Nothing feels true when I put it down on paper. It just feels like a *part* of a truth, and *part* of a truth is a lie. Or something like that. I don't know how else to explain it except to say that right now it's easier not to try than to feel like I'm telling a lie. I'm too tired to write, anyhow. I'm back at the day-care center, being Dizzy Lizzy. I do at least like my job. The kids are great, and we get to spend lots of time out-of-doors. It's been so pretty lately, with everything green and flowering. I hope you get outside sometimes.

Here are all the letters. Looking at them gives me the oddest feeling—both sad and happy. Now you can answer them—soon!

Love,
Liz

Dear Liz,

Your interpretation of my poem astonished me. I don't think I understood it so
well myself. Yes, it says what you think it
says. How can you have learned and understood, at your age, that there are only "stories without endings"? You're so strong, and
bright, Liz. Lord, how I have missed you.

I've been reading your letters, over and
over again. I can't wait until we can sit down
and talk about things—what it was like for
you at Shana's and how things are with
Kelly and which colleges you should visit.
But I hate seeing how much I alarmed you
by disappearing the way I did.

The thing that touched me most about
your letters was how much you seem to
count on me to have some sort of "wisdom." I don't, Liz. Not anymore. Or not
yet. But you have plenty of your own. Learn
to rely on that and to listen to yourself. If I
had, I could never have drifted so far off
course. That's the only wisdom I'm sure of

now. You mustn't idolize me. No person is perfect. Life is too complex for that.

And please, no more talk of guilt or right and wrong between us. I assure you, the fault was all on my side. I drew you, a hungering adolescent, into my life at a time when I was hungering also, and that wasn't right. I was the adult. Your behavior was more than admirable and responsible, which makes mine all the more reprehensible. Still, some part of me can't help thinking that in many ways perhaps things simply unfolded as they were intended to unfold. We've both grown from what's happened, so how can we not rejoice in it a little? Let's not think anymore of past pain, but only move forward and go on caring about each other.

It's interesting, what you've felt about there being no "right" way of seeing, and of course it's true. The ground *is* always shifting and a person's perception depends so much on where she's standing. But isn't that precisely the job of the artist—to capture that shifting ground? You can write from Elspeth's viewpoint, but you can also write from her father's, and that broadens the picture.

I'm rereading an old favorite, which I haven't read in years—Virginia Woolf's *To the Lighthouse*. Do you know it? It's such a wonderful book. The central image is the lighthouse, whose beacon goes round and around—light and then darkness, light and then darkness, and on and on. Constant, eternal flux, but at the center always the steady lighthouse. Virginia Woolf is the master at catching the shifting ground. You will be too someday.

I think you should visit me soon. Just be prepared—my hands still shake. My doctor says it's the medication, but I'm not completely convinced. They reflect the way I feel. As I grow calmer at my center, the world outside of me seems to tilt and I can't quite latch onto it. I know I will, though. Now and then I catch a glimpse of the lighthouse. Or maybe I *am* the lighthouse—now there's a thought!

By the way, I didn't sell my parents' house. I'm going to go home and live in it and do some writing. Who knows? I might have money coming in from a book or two

by the time my inheritance runs out and I
can settle in as an old-lady Southern author.
Wouldn't that be bliss?

Love,
Julia

July 16, 1996

Dear Julia,

How can you say you don't have wisdom, when every line you write is full of it? You're going to become a writer, I can feel it. You'll write stories without endings, that lead people out of their locked-in world and onto a bigger, wider path that winds on forever, into a kind of beautiful eternity.

I do know what you mean though about life being complex. I used to think that somewhere out there it wasn't, that life and people *could* be perfect. Now I'm becoming interested in just the opposite. It's sort of beautiful to me how Dad tries to deal with all of his flaws. (Did I just say that?) I remember how I used to think there were two of me—the

who lived in the
why did it never
t be two of other
n see and the
rivate? Or that
o of anyone, but
ed people.

And delicate pink flowers
And a chip
Because it's old

Liz also has a teapot
Shaped like a heart
She tips—
It pours
And fills her cup
With quiet
Sparkling
Art

Oh, Liz, hope is everywhere. Can't you just feel it? See you soon.

Love,
Julia

Dear Journal,

Yes, I can feel the hope. It's everywhere, just like Julia says. Hope that Julia will get better and get to live in her house in Virginia. Hope that my parents will actually learn to be happy. Hope that I'll go to college and someday become a writer—a *real* writer who can "catch the shifting ground." Until that happens you're only the Journal of Dizzy Lizzy Who Is Doing the Best She Can. But Journal—that's not so bad.